MAVERICK MARSHAL

Nelson Nye

He was just a no-account cowhand. Then they pinned a tin star on his chest and he was the law. They swore him in quicker than lightning and didn't expect him to live long enough to pocket his first pay. After all, what chance did a green-as-grass cowpoke have against the killer they called Tularosa?

But now Frank Carrico was gunned for justice. And he was going to clean up South Fork with bullets and fists. Because the young lawman was crazy enough to try . . . and good enough to succeed!

NELSON NYE

Maverick Marshal,

John Curley & Associates, Inc.
South Yarmouth, Ma.

Library of Congress Cataloging-in-Publication Data

Nye, Nelson C. (Nelson Coral), 1907–
  Maverick marshal.

  1. Large type books.   I. Title.
[PS3527.Y33M38 1988]   813′.54   88–1185
ISBN 1–55504–588–X (lg. print)
ISBN 1–55504–571–5 (pbk. : lg. print)

Published in Large Print by arrangement with Donald MacCampbell, Inc. in the United States and Canada; the U.K. and British Commonwealth and the rest of the world market.

Distributed in the U.K. and Commonwealth by Chivers Book Sales Limited.

Printed in Great Britain

CHAPTER ONE

It began with a big temptation – too big for a man like Frank to resist no matter what trouble it might run him into. Turbulence and violence had given him a rep. He knew that it was the bold men in this world who got their names in the pot. He also knew with his first sight of the town that he was never going back to punching cows for old Sam Church.

In a place like South Fork, which was a jumping-off point for outfits heading up the trail to Dodge City, a person had to be born on the right side of Gurden's saloon or be a part of the scum for the rest of his natural. Such, at least, was the established tradition. Now Frank saw a way of changing all that.

He was going to wake this place up!

Marshal of South Fork, he breathed, and reared back his shoulders.

He grinned as he thought of Honey Kimberland. Smallest waist, biggest smile, yellowest hair of any girl in the country; and as far above Frank as the damn moon – but there wasn't no law against dreaming.

1

She had been in Frank's mind ever since the day he'd hauled her out of that south-shore boghole where she'd run just in time to miss the horns of Church's bull. Frank had cut down the bull with his pistol (and worked half the next winter getting its cost off the books) before he'd realized it wasn't about to go into that muck even for a tidbit as tempting as Honey.

Four years ago – Lord how time flew! Frank wondered if she remembered, being not much over fifteen when he'd saved her. He recollected the look of her knees with the mud on them, and the way she had clung to him shivering and shaking. She'd been well filled out even then and he remembered the clean woman smell of her hair.... He remembered too damn well, he thought wryly.

It was nearly full dark and the nighthawks were swooping when he came into town and worked his dun horse through the Saturday night crush. He put the animal up to the pole fronting Gurden's Saloon and sat a spell having his look along the street. Frank was a big fellow and a rough one with his burly brawler's shoulders. And yet someway, strangely, he was a little reluctant about the marshal's job, thinking back to that talk he'd had with John Arnold. Arnold, one of the town councilmen, was a man grown old in the cow game, closest to being tolerant of any of the local big owners.

"But why me?" Frank had asked when Arnold let it be known the Town Council was dissatisfied with the man they'd fetched in from outside to pack their tin. "Ashenfeldt's a tophand at this pistol-packing business. All I know is cows."

Arnold, smiling, shifted his cud. "You've made your mark in this town as a real scraperoo. It's these local sports who've put the skids under Joe. They won't try that with you – they'll know better. Besides," Arnold said, warming up to his subject, "you're ambitious."

Frank scowled. But it was true enough, he supposed. If he was ever to make any impression on Honey it was time he got known for something besides brawling and shoving cows' tails around. Still it wasn't a job he would voluntarily have gone after. He knew the riptide of pressures by which things around here were made to suit the big owners and could not resist taking a sly poke at the rancher. "You hunting a dog that'll come to your whistle?"

The tightening of Arnold's hands showed the shaft had gone home, but he said easy enough, "We've got to have a man who

3

understands local conditions, one who'll know when to reach and when to leave well enough alone. You fit that to a T."

"What's old Church think about it?"

"I haven't talked to Church about it; the deal is up to the Town Council. Pay is one-twenty a month. I could put it into cows for you, Frank."

It would be obliging Arnold to take the marshal's job, which meant it probably would suit Honey Kimberland's old man too. Kimberland generally pulled most of the strings that got pulled. Without at least his tacit approval a man wouldn't look to get anywhere at all here. W. T. Kimberland *was* South Fork – and his daughter wouldn't be marrying any thirty-a-month cowhand.

Frank took a deep breath. "How do you know I can have the damned job?"

Arnold said quietly, "Push it around for a while in your mind. Council won't meet before Saturday night. If you want to take a whirl at it, come in."

So here he was, and it was Saturday night with the dust and the racket boiling out of the street and the town crammed with men who would just as lief gutshoot a tinbadge as look at him.

Among the mounds of stored goods in the back room of the Mercantile, Krantz, who

4

owned the place, sat around with the other two Councilmen, sourly nursing their secret antagonisms, paying little attention to the voices out front where his weary clerks, wishing mightily to be done, tramped about the gabbing customers, reaching down and stacking purchases absent-mindedly ordered between bursts of gossip.

Krantz pushed an already soggy bandana across the moist shine of his completely bald head. He said, "I don't like it."

Chip Gurden, who owned the Opal and could generally be counted on to front for the riffraff and drifters, sighed. "Seems like I remember you sayin' that." His glance sawed at Krantz's nerves. The storekeeper jumped up, frustratedly fidgeting and popping his knuckles while his eyes slewed irascibly from one to the other of them. "That roughneck! How can ve trust our lives yet, und our goots, to such a one?"

Gurden's saloonkeeper's face in the light of the lamps showed no more expression than one of his table checks.

Arnold said, "He'll be all right."

Krantz, swinging back, sat down heavily. "Yah! All right for you cow people! What about the rest of us?"

"If he don't stay in line, two votes from

5

this Council will take the tin away from him," said Arnold.

Gurden nodded. He fetched a black stogie from a case and bit the end off. He considered it a moment, scratched a match and fired up. "That's for sure," he said dryly. He broke the match and put his foot on it.

"I don't like it," Krantz repeated.

"Vote against him then," Arnold suggested smoothly.

Gurden growled through the smoke, "Maybe Frank's got other fish to fry. We been here twenty minutes already."

Arnold said to Krantz, "You're the Clerk of this outfit. Call the meeting adjourned if it'll make you feel any better."

Krantz glared, affronted. "You talk like you was Kimberland. You know this – this *wildman* will look out for your interests. Py Gott! Gurden has bouncers. Me, all I got iss a fortune in breakables und a pair of scairt clerks! Ve got to haf some law in this –"

Someone's fist banged heavily against the door.

Krantz, still fuming, got up and unbarred it. Frank Carrico came in and heard the door slammed behind him. "So you're here!" Krantz scowled. Frank looked at the other two. "Thought I was expected."

6

"Begun to think you weren't coming." Arnold shoved a keg out.

Frank, settling his back to the wall, searched Gurden's face. "This deal suit you?"

"I'll string along."

"Yah – you got bouncers!" Krantz, with his head up like a dog catching wolf smell, demanded of Frank bitterly: "You understandt this chob do you?"

"Expect I could make out to get a line on it." Frank, knowing Krantz didn't like him, considered the storekeeper, grinning a little. "Main thing, I reckon, is to keep you fellers in business, ain't it?"

"Iss something funny? Why you grin? Ve got troubles – wild-eyed crazy galoots wit pistols. Py Gott, ve need protection! Las' night these trail hands wreck Fantshon's blace like a pig vind!"

"Where was your badge toter?" asked Frank.

"He done the best he could," Gurden said.

Arnold, clearing his throat, suggested getting down to business. Frank stared at the rancher, trying to lay hold of something. Top dogs in South Fork acknowledged no one but W. T. Kimberland and it was gnawing at Frank's mind that Arnold would be acting for W. T. right now.

Krantz blew out his cheeks and glared about him dismally, his look lingering longest on the face of the saloonkeeper. Gurden gave him no encouragement. Krantz swabbed his baldness again with the wadded bandanna and testily said, "Comes now Frank Carrico, a candidate for marshal. All in favor signify by saying 'aye'."

"Aye." That was Arnold, looking smug and mighty virtuous. Gurden's slow nod held a hint of wry humor.

Krantz said bitterly, "Lift your right hand and put the other on this book."

After Frank was sworn in he pocketed the keys the storekeeper gave him and picked up the paper on which were set forth the duties of his office, local ordinances and so forth. His glance went to Arnold. "Where's the badge?"

"We'll step over to Ben's" Arnold murmured.

Ben Holliday ran the local furniture emporium. When there was call for it he also furnished caskets at three times the actual cost. There could only be one reason, Frank reflected, for going to Ben's. He took a tighter grip on himself going over there, but when he stood with the others staring down at Ashenfeldt's body, he couldn't restrain a

8

shiver. Peering at Arnold he said: "Who did it?"

Gurden's grin was thin and crooked. "Make a guess."

"Some drunken trail hand?"

"One of Draicup's crowd," Arnold said. Frank's eyes slitted.

Krantz said, "didn't you know they vas back?"

"Which one?" Frank asked, sounding like something had got stuck in his windpipe. Three months ago, in a drunken brawl, Frank had smashed a heap of glass in Gurden's Opal bar.

The saloonkeeper now, with the re-membrance of this coming alive on his cheeks, said, "Tularosa," and showed a huge enjoyment. "Maybe that star don't look so good to you now."

Frank reached down and got the tin from the dead man's vest. With his face hard as rock he fastened it onto his shirt front. His eyes cut at Arnold. "Draicup's crew still around?"

"Tularosa's here. Fetched in a wagon with a busted hub and him and another's laying over to wait for it."

Krantz, ever fearful of violence, said, "you can have the exbense of vun deputy – up to,

9

that is, fifty dollars a month. If you haf to bay more it comes out of your bocket."

"How free a hand have I got with this job?"

Arnold said, "In what way?"

Frank waved the paper the storekeeper had given him. "This part about guns. Man would need an army to disarm every ranny that comes into this town."

"You asked for it." That was Gurden.

Arnold fingered his thin mustache. "What do you have in mind, Frank?"

"It's the rotgut," Franks said, "that puts these boys on the prod."

The sardonic enjoyment fell off Gurden's face. "Now wait a minute! If you think for one –"

"I was going to suggest," Frank said mildly, "that whenever they come into a place where they can buy it we make it a rule their guns must be checked at the bar. I'll undertake to make that stick."

"It would help," Krantz said, brightening.

Arnold nodded.

Chip Gurden said grudgingly, "I'll go along on that," and got up. "What are you figurin' to do about Tularosa?"

"What do you want me to do?"

"He killed somebody, didn't he? Put the sonofabitch in jail!"

10

Draicup, held to be rougher than a cob, hailed from someplace down in the brasada. He'd been here before and always drove a mixed herd which was road-branded Spur. He packed a thick wallet crammed with powers of attorney and had taken twenty thousand cattle up to Dodge. His passing last year had cost the town four men – three of these killed by this same Tularosa.

Knowing all this, considering it, Frank stood on Ben's steps and scowlingly eyed the street. Up till now he'd thought only of Honey and the prestige of being the Law in this town. Now he was forced to look at other things, the town itself, the obligations of this job, and he had his moment of dark, grim wonder.

Ranch hands, trail hands, tramped the scarred walks and stopped in clotted knots of drab color wherever they came across friends or an argument. Staring over the heads of this noisy throng, over the collection of rigs and paintless wagons wedged cheek by jowl into that restive line of stamping, tail-switching rein-tied horses, Frank's glance prowled the street's far side with some care.

Most of the whiskey was consumed in three places, all of them on Frank's side of

11

the street. Directly across loomed the Hays Hotel. East, to the left of the place as Frank faced it and separated only by a vacant lot, was the stage depot, horse barns and Halbertson's hay shed. West of the hotel was the jail and marshal's quarters, Fentriss' livery with its pole corrals – a growing establishment doing considerable business at this time of the year catering to drovers. Next west was the Chuckwagon where a stove-up Church cowhand eked out a living cooking for those who cared for that kind of grub; he had plenty of vacant space on both sides of him. Farther west – the last building – was the blacksmith shop. Beyond was just grass, a ragged chewed and trampled sea of it, bed grounds of the trail herds.

On this side where Frank stood, dividing the respectable and sinful sides of it, was Gurden's Opal Bar, hangout of horsemen, mecca of those wild ones howling up out of the south. Beyond Gurden's, looking west, was Bernie's gun shop, a pool hall with a red-lettered, Billiards, chipped and peeling across its front and, west of this, the Blue Flag saloon, another vacant lot, then Minnie's place, the wrecked Fantshon store and Trench Brothers lumber.

East of Gurden's, separated from it by no more than the width of Krantz's wagon pass, was the Mercantile where Frank had just been to meet with the Council and latch onto this job John Arnold had got him. Next in line was Ben's Furniture (where Frank stood now), Pete's Tonsorial Parlor, the New York Cafe where drummers and comparable local fry did their nooning, the Bon Ton Millinery, a bake shop run by a Swede from Istanbul, and Wolverton's Saddlery.

A little beyond, dubbed 'Snob Holler' by the bunk-house fraternity, were the homes of the merchants and socially elite. Clerks and artisans lived on the south side in a heterogeneous muddle of shacks congregated beyond Halbertson's hay shed. Behind the town, north of it, were the barrens leading into the Claybank Hills; between barrens and hills swirled the opaque crimson waters of the river that gave South Fork its name.

Peering again southwest toward the holding grounds Frank considered the dark mass of close-bunched cattle, knowing these would have no connection with Draicup whose own stock would now be strung out on the trail. This was an outfit just lately arrived, peaceful-seeming in the night but sure to have dumped more strange riders on the town.

Frank hauled Tularosa out of the back of this survey where he'd been crouched, emptily grinning. Frank had only bumped into the fellow once and had privately hoped never to see him again. Six feet four, rawboned and gangling – so thin, as someone put it, he could have crawled through the eye of a needle and "never got one damn hair outa place." The odd thing was that, except for his eyes, he didn't look like a killer. He had a lantern-jawed dished-up sort of a face framing clackety store teeth and a spatter of freckles. He was a queer guy to look at – with that wistfully sober kind of bewildered expression frequently glimpsed on small boys called up for a lecture. Inside he was nothing but a bundle of nerves, unpredictable, explosive as capped dynamite.

Frank reckoned himself seven kinds of a fool to take the job but turned west up the street, alert to each shape that dragged its spurs through the dust. Without sighting his quarry he pushed through the batwings into Gruden's Opal Bar, braced against the racket that rolled against him like a wave.

All the games were in full swing. Men stood bellying the bar six deep. There were a lot of strange faces but not the one he was hunting. A couple of men suddenly flanked him, grinning. One of these was Kelly, a man Frank had used to punch cows with – narrow-chested, fiddle footed, always looking

14

for something he didn't have, but a fair enough hand in a pinch or a bender.

"Man," Kelly said, "you're sure stickin' your neck out!"

Frank passed it off and shot a glance at the other one. This was Gurden's chief bouncer, a fellow called "Mousetrap" who would tip the scales at about 280 and fancied himself pretty slick with a gun. He was new around here, a recent investment on the part of Chip Gurden.

"Better sign me up, Frank," Kelly said, "while you're able."

Frank grinned and, using his elbows, moved up to the bar.

Scowls twisted faces colored by resentment. Frank picked up a bottle and thumped the bar top for attention. Turning his back against the wood he faced the packed room and called out, "As of twelve noon tomorrow there will be no pistols carried where whisky is served. All guns will be left with the barkeep. That's a new town ordinance and it's going to be enforced."

He went out through an ominous silence.

The night felt cold against his face. He felt a chill digging into the small of his back.

Bill Grace, Kimberland's range boss, came along with a couple of punchers, showing no surprise at the sight of Frank's star. He stared up at Frank's face with the briefest of glances, jerked a nod and went on. The punchers looked back. Frank saw one of them grinning.

Cutting around the Blue Flat he stepped in through the rear, still without catching sight of Tularosa. He stood a bit, thinking. The fellow might be over at Minnie's or following his bent in the dark of some alley. He might be at the blacksmith's or feeding his face in the New York Cafe, though this last was out of bounds. Frank found himself listening for gunshots.

The Flag didn't have as much flash as Gurden's which flaunted framed women without clothes above its bar and a bevy of live ones not clad a heap warmer. This place wasn't as noisy though money was changing hands pretty regular. Young Church, old Sam's son, was at the bar getting rapidly plastered. Arrogance lay in the flash of his stare and when he saw Frank a surge of roan color rushed into his cheeks. He pushed away from the bar, still carrying his bottle, and reeled toward Frank.

Frank said, "Hello, Will."

Eyes ugly, Will Church floundered to a stop three feet away and glared belligerently. He indulged the manners of a drunken hidalgo surveying a truant peon. "You were told to stay out there at Bospero Flats."

"That's right," Frank said.

"Then why ain't you out there? You think those cows'll stay hitched without watching'?"

Some of the nearer noise began to dim away as men twisted around or looked up from their cards. Frank's eyes flattened a little. "If they're worryin' you, Will, perhaps you'd better go see to them." Frank's hand brushed the star that was pinned to his shirtfront.

The wink of the metal suddenly caught Church's attention. He showed a sultry surprise. His mouth twisted with fury as men back of him shifted, the sound of this seeming as a goad to his temper. As heir apparent to the second largest spread in the country young Church wasn't accustomed to being talked back at. His cheeks began to burn. He had never liked Frank anyway.

Frank, smiling meagerly, was turning away when Church lunged for him, lifting the bottle. Frank's head whipped around. Ducking under the bottle he came up, tight with outrage, hammering four knuckles to the point of Church's chin. It sounded like a bat knocking a ball over the fence.

Church's head snapped back with all his

features screwed together. The off-balanced weight of chest and head abruptly toppled him. He hit the floor on his back and skidded into the bar, the bottle jaggedly breaking against the brass foot rail.

Will Church climbed to his feet groggily shaking his head. He discovered the splattered whisky and his stare, coming up, found Frank. He let out a shout and came at Frank with the bottle neck.

Church was big, even bigger than Frank, with a bulging swell of chest and arm and the hatred of balked arrogance baring his teeth. He shortened his grip on the neck of the bottle to give more reach to the jagged shard. He looked like an ape above the glitter of the glass.

Frank asked quietly, "Sure you want to go on with this, Will?"

Church showed the brawn of a gorilla and about as much reason as he stood there shifting his weight, breathing heavily. Men were crowding in through the batwings as word of the fight ran down the street. Frank got hold of the back of a chair.

"Mind the mirrors!" the barkeep yelled. Somebody's laugh was a sound of hysteria. The faces around Frank grew tense and avid as he brought the chair up in front of him.

Now Will leaped, throwing up a hand to

ward off the chair, attempting to dive in under it. One spur hooked into the cloth of a pant's leg and he went down, cursing viciously. Frank, prodded by past injustices, brought the chair up over his head; but something stayed him and he reluctantly stepped back, allowing the man to regain his feet.

It was while Church was trying to get up that the racket of shots came – five of them, close-spaced, whipping Frank around, scowling.

He let go of the chair. The batwings were blocked by a solid crush of onlookers. He put his weight against the edge of the crowd. "Make way!" He shoved the nearest man roughly, driving broad shoulders into the wedge, hurling them back with the ram of his elbows.

Someone swung at him, knocking his hat off. He could feel them stiffening. A man swung at Frank, yelling wickedly. Frank hurled him back into the crowd with black fury. He tore the gun from a fist and beat his way clear with it, leaving behind the wild sound of their temper. He stumbled into the night, his shirt hanging in ribbons.

He ran around the back end of the pool hall and came into Gurden's with the gun still in hand. He backed out almost at once, finding no sign of trouble, sprinting down the passage between the Opal and Bernie's gun shop. Coming onto the walk he caught the sharp bark of two additional shots and swore in exasperation. It was nothing more alarming than a string of whooping ranch hands letting go at the moon as they roared out of town.

Frank threw the pistol away and remembered his hat. For ten years that hat had been a part of himself but he didn't go back after it. He tramped instead into the Mercantile and bought himself a new one, black this time, and a dark shield-fronted shirt, going – out of deference to female shoppers – into the back room to get into it.

Coming out he looked around, hoping to catch a glimpse of Honey, having noticed a Bar 40 wagon out front. While he was looking Krantz grabbed his elbow. "You get him?"

"Get who?"

"Tularosa." The lamps' shine winked off the thick lenses of the storekeeper's spectacles. "He vas in mine blace."

Frank, swearing, bundled the discarded shirt into Krantz's hands and hurried through the front door. He stopped under the overhang, avoiding the stippling of light from the windows. He found it hard to make out anyone, what with so much in shadow and all the dust stirred up by the traffic. He looked for five minutes and decided to try Minnie's.

He got his horse from the rack, the big dun he'd come in on, a *bayo coyote* with black mane and tail and a stripe down its spine in addition to smudges about the knees. A black horse in this job would have probably been smarter but Frank, like most of those who rode after cattle, was sold on duns, particularly duns with zebra marks descended from the toughest Spanish stock in the land.

Still riled with himself Frank got into the saddle and pointed the horse toward the west end of town.

Minnie was a character, practically an institution. A lot of folks would have liked to see her moved but she had, in Frank's mind, as much right to her business as anybody else. She kept an orderly house, which was more than could be said for the likes of Chip Gurden. More he thought about the place the more convinced Frank became that he would find his man holed up there. Tularosa made no secret of his affinity for the ladies.

All the shades were drawn but there were horses at the tie rail – two roans, a paint and three sorrels. Frank tied the dun and took a last look behind him. He ducked under the rail and felt to see if he had his pistol, resettling its barrel lightly, not hankering for anything to balk his need if he were forced to put hand to it.

He drew off his dark thoughts and pulled open the door.

CHAPTER TWO

This layout had once been a food stop on the overland stage line between Elk City and Dalhart, and the face-lifting Minnie had given the joint had not greatly changed its flavor. The big room Frank stepped into had all the look of a stage stop bar. She had got the place cheap when town expansion had decided the company to remove to a site directly across from the New York Cafe.

The old potbellied stove still held its key spot in the middle of things. The scarred pine bar took up most of the left wall, the wall across from it being cut by three doors. No mirrors, no pictures; five kitchen chairs were racked before the north wall, the south wall was set up similarly except that here only two of the five were empty. Strangers held down the other three, men Frank had never run into before. None of them much resembled Tularosa beyond their big hats, brush-scarred boots and the gun-weighted cartridge belts strapped about their middles.

Frank, after that one sweeping glance, darkly stared at the three closed doors to his right. The nearest, he remembered, let into the woodshed. The farther, opening onto closed stairs, gave access to the rooms above. It was the middle door that held his attention. It led directly outside behind the screen of the woodshed and was a means of escape for men embarrassed to be found here.

Frank, ducking out, left the door standing open and ran around the shed's bulk, eyes expectant, gun in hand. But if there was anyone lurking in these shadows he didn't see them. Holstering his gun, he went back inside, ignoring the truculent looks the men gave him.

Minnie's raw Irish voice came from back of the bar. "Whativer are ye doin' a-runnin' around me place like a banshee?"

She was a big coarse-boned woman with an orange-colored pompadour untidily bushed above crimson cheeks. Thirty years ago she might have been handsome but time had taken away this advantage; she had given up bemoaning or bothering about it. She was interested in one thing – cash, like the rest of them. "What's that ye've got on yer shirtfront, Frank? Don't be tellin' me ye've turned plumb fool at last."

Frank grinned a little sheepishly, rubbed the palms of his hands against the thighs of his pants. "Any redheads around?"

"Redheads, is it?" She was watching him shrewdly. "I got the one from Saint Looey, if that's who ye're meanin'. I figured after the –"

"I'm not talking about fillies."

"Then ye're in the wrong stall. Do yer huntin' some other place."

Frank swung around. "What outfit you fellers with?"

Resentment was plain in the cut of their eyes. Minnie said, giving him the flat of her tongue. "Don't be rowellin' me guests, ye dom star-packin' blatherskite!" But after a moment the smallest one said, "Gourd an' Vine. Out of Corpus."

"Get shucked of that hardware if you come into town tomorrow. You can't go heeled in any place that sells whisky. Including this dive." Frank went out.

He could, of course, have searched the place, but not without laying up trouble. If Tularosa was here he'd have to come out.

Frank got on his horse. He scowled, knowing he couldn't afford to hang fire here. He had the whole town to patrol and the riskiest hours were still ahead.

He breathed a sigh into the darkness and swore irascibly. It was in his mind the Council had jobbed him, keeping Tularosa back until he'd taken the oath. Yet in fairness he had to admit he couldn't blame them. Nobody would have touched this job with a prod pole if it had been aired Tularosa was the first thing on the docket. The man was like a wild animal.

Frank shook his head and cursed again, and observed Danny Settles shuffling along with his sack, threadbare coat flapping around bony legs as he picked a muttering way toward the Mercantile. Probably going after groceries, trying to reach the doors before Krantz locked up.

Perhaps because he was a loner himself, Frank had always had a soft place in his heart for Danny Settles who was the nearest thing South Fork had to a halfwit. He had a cave or a burrow somewhere out in the Barrens. It was the measure of his queerness that he made pets of crawling varmints. He'd been around as long as Frank could remember, the butt of coarse jokes and a lot of fool horseplay, a wizard at repairing firearms and the credulity of a child. He pieced out a precarious existence doing exacting odd jobs for Bernie, the gunsmith, while waiting for the monthly pittance mailed West by his father, a Boston industrialist who had gone to great lengths to be shed of him. He was the result, it was said, of too much education.

Frank's thoughts went resentfully back to John Arnold. Arnold and Gurden had played him for a sucker. There was no doubt about it. They'd known Ashenfeldt was dead, and by whose hand, when they'd set this up for him.

He was mad enough to shove the damned badge down their throats. Yet even as this occurred to him Frank saw in his mind the face and shape of Honey Kimberland and licked parched lips. The one good thing, Frank guessed, in his life. Actually, he supposed, he'd ought to thank the damned Council for giving him this chance. But, hating abysmally to be maneuvered, he scowled at the dust-fogged shine of the Opal, knowing it was Gurden who'd kept Tularosa hidden till they'd got Frank clinched into the job. Chip Gurden had known Frank couldn't back down after that.

Frank yanked his six-shooter savagely out of its leather and let the dun carry him across the hundred-foot width of the hoof-tracked road.

The blacksmith was still working by the light of a lantern. Frank, cutting around to come up from the holding grounds, caught the iron-dulled strokes of his hammer. Frank heard the mumble of voices as he moved up on the door. He walked the dun into the light of the lanterns, seeing the smith bent over his bellows and the squatted-down shape of a cow wrangler watching him. He was an old coot, this trail hand, weathered and wrinkled as a chucked-away boot. Frank, eyeing the both of them, spoke to the smith. "You got that hub ready yet for Draicup's wagon?"

The smith's head came around. "Why, hello, Frank. Just about, I guess."

"Don't turn loose of it till I give you the word."

The smith and that other one traded quick glances.

"I'm a-waitin' on thet wheel, son," the squatted gent said mildly.

This meekness didn't deceive Frank. There wasn't one trail hand in twenty who was not plumb willing, night or day, to tackle his weight in wildcats. Frank said to the trail hand:

"Slide out of that shell belt."

The mild eyes measured him.

The smith said nervously, "Man, that's Frank Carrico!"

The old man, grunting, finally let the belt drop.

"Want I should git it fer you, Frank?" the smith asked.

"Just hang onto that wheel till I tell you different." Frank backed his dun out of the light from the door.

He'd been lucky! There was sweat all over him. His hands got to shaking till he had to grab hold of the horn to keep them quiet when he thought of what a fool he'd been to go and brace that jigger with his back wide open. If Tularosa had come up or been around someplace watching – Frank bitterly swore.

He picked up his reins and sent the dun toward the street. A glance swiveled over his shoulder at Minnie's revealed nothing suspicious. He drew a ragged breath. Worry could do a man in sure as anything! He fetched his face around for a look at the Chuckwagon. It was off there ahead of him, its canvas top a dirty blur against the lantern beneath its fly.

He fetched Honey back into mind, recalling the soft exciting feel of her with her heart pounding wildly and the smell of her tumbled hair whipping round him. The job was worth this risk if it would do what he wanted.

He wasn't sure it would. But let him once get this town to eating out of his hand and a proper respect slapped into these trail crews and he guessed not many doors would stay shut against him.

This was still a young land where what you did was more important than who you were or where you'd come from. Old W. T. wasn't a man to forget that. If half the stories were true *his* start wouldn't bear much looking into either.

Frank was forty yards from the subdued shine of the flapping canvas when he became aware of the stopped wagon. There was a girl holding the reins, and a horse-backer talking to her. This was about all Frank could make out, the moon being under a cloud at the moment. A little wind had sprung up, whipping their words away. He likely wouldn't have noticed them at all if he had been less edgy and they hadn't been caught against the light from the Blue Flag.

With Honey on his mind they took immediate hold of his interest. He kneed the dun toward them, remembering the wagon from Bar 40 at the Mercantile. He got nearer. He saw the girl shake her head and sway away from the fellow, saw the man's arm

29

come up as he bent after her from the saddle. The girl reached for the whip. Snorting contemptuously, the fellow grabbed her.

Frank didn't wait to see any more. He slammed the dun into the other man's mount, catching him by the coat at the shoulder, yanking him back with an uncaring roughness that mighty near dumped him onto the ground. "Ma'am, is this galoot bothering you?"

In Frank's grip the man, who seemed to be on the bony side, was in no position to do much of anything, suspended as he was halfway out of the saddle. His horse snorted nervously, dancing a little.

"Why, no, not particularly." Her voice was pleasant. It wasn't Honey's. She was new here. She didn't seem much excited – appeared more like she was smiling. It kind of made Frank feel foolish.

Perhaps she sensed his resentment. "I wouldn't want you to drop him under those hoofs."

Frank very nearly did. For, just then, the moon came out. The fellow twisted his head, and Frank felt like Jonah in the belly of the whale.

The "galoot" he had hold of was Tularosa.

Frank had time only to realize this – when young Church, taut with fury, yelled:

"Frank!"

Frank saw the glint of metal in Church's lifting hand. Tularosa began to struggle, trying to get leverage, trying to pull his far leg across the drag of the saddle. Frank was in a bad spot. He slapped the gunfighter savagely. Then he growled at Church, "Will, keep out of this."

"Don't use that tone on me, you bastard!"

Frank half turned the frozen mask of his face. In that fleeting fragment of time his mind absorbed details without conscious understanding or realization of it even: the still look of the girl, the forward clump of Church's boots, the collecting crowd closing in about them. Yet never for an instant did Frank's glance quit the man he had hold of. While Church in his drunken fury might shoot, there was not the slightest question about Tularosa. The moment that sidewinder got any leverage he'd latch onto a gun and he would damn sure use it.

The strain of keeping his grip, of holding the fellow off balance, was beginning to play hell with the muscles of Frank's arm. He could hear Church coming up and, made hollow by the torture of this impasse, he rammed a knee into Tularosa's chest. It fetched a grunt from the redhead, but too much of Frank's strength was concentrated

31

on holding him. The blow did nothing to ease the deadlock that was pushing Frank toward the brink of disaster.

He sensed the girl was in motion. He made a desperate attempt to reach Tularosa's holstered pistol, but the grip that kept Tularosa from trying also balked Frank. The saddle-horn prevented Frank from reaching his own.

The girl cried: "Keep out of this!" and snatched up her whip. Frank heard the snarl of Church's breath. The thump of his stride broke around the near end of the wagon.

"I'm goin' to cut you down to size!" Church sheezed.

Frank's left hand, fisting, hit Tularosa on the side of the face. He struck once more but he couldn't get steam enough into the punches.

The gunfighter grated, "I'll remember you, mister," and tried again to get a boot braced against his saddle.

With the flat of his hand Frank cracked Tularosa across the bridge of the nose. The man yelled. Church fired. Tularosa's horse squealed and, flinging its head down, went to pitching. The gun-fighter's legs lost contact and the dropped sprawl of his weight dragged Frank off the dun.

They fell into a dust-streaked haze of

flying hoofs. Frank lost the man. The smothery stench of powdered earth enveloped them and through this fog Frank glimpsed the bobbling approach of a lantern. The dim grumble of Church's steady cursing was lost in the racket of hoofs and shouts. Frank's need to relocate the killer became more acute with each passing instant. It was then, as Frank came onto his knees, that he discovered the full meaning of the word 'desperation'. In the fall or the rolling he had lost his gun.

He swayed aside, barely avoiding the lashing hoof of a horse. The dust was so thick he couldn't see two yards in front of him. His face and clothing were gritty with the stuff, his burning eyes were filled with tears. He faintly heard the girl cry out, and he was groping blindly toward her when hardly beyond the stretch of his hand a man sharply screamed. Frank's legs crashed into something yielding, upending him. Back of him someplace a gun's report bludgeoned out of the uproar.

The dust started clearing in an updraft of air. Horses and men materialized out of it and patches of oil-yellow light from the store fronts. He caught the shape of the wagon with the girl standing in it. Someone yelled, *"There he is!"* and Frank flung himself around just as Church fired again.

Frank came out of that crouch with a wildly furious swing that took Church full in the wind. Frank gave the big ranchman no time to recover but tore into him with a ferocity that drove Church back into the crowd. Frank jerked the gun from Church's grip and whacked him across the neck with the butt of it. Church yelled and Frank hit him again. Still yelling, Church fell.

Coughing, wheezing from dust and exertion, Frank saw the lantern throw its shine on Church's face. The crowd stood silent. One cheek showed a welt like a brand burn where Frank had struck him and there was a red streak of blood against the side of his neck. Church wasn't out but he was considerably more cautious. He finally squirmed over and was helped to his feet by some of the crowd.

Nothing Will Church did would have surprised Frank much. Old Sam, Will's sire, was a tight-fisted miser, and Will's mother was a cowed little wisp of a woman who never opened her mouth unless spoken to. In the five years Frank had ridden for Circle C (doing the work of a foreman on the pay of a horse wrangler) he'd never seen Mrs.

Church let go of two words without first peering at Sam or Will for permission.

Young Will shook his shoulders together, glance bright with venom as he twisted his head from one side to the other. "You ain't done with this," he said thickly. "Gimme that gun."

"You ain't got sense enough to pack a gun, damn you. If you ever fetch another one into this town I'll lock you up like any other nuisance. Now get going," Frank growled, swinging away from him.

Men stepped back. Frank found his new hat and picked it up, cuffing the dust off. The outer fringes of the crowd began to dissolve in search of other amusement. The girl's voice called, "Marshal –"

Frank walked over. "You all right, Miss?"

She eyed him curiously. "Of course. You won't need that gun to speak with me."

Frank looked down at Church's pistol and put it away. The remains of his anger was still reflected in his cheeks and the weight of regret over losing Tularosa sawed across his morose thoughts till he glanced up and found her smiling. He looked more closely then, for the first time really seeing her.

She was not the kind a man would easily forget. She had shape and there was an attraction of some kind emanating from her that compelled his sharpest interest. It was like a current running between them. Her voice took hold of him too. She said, "I haven't thanked you –"

"No thanks called for, Miss."

He saw the flash of her teeth and, annoyed with himself, decided her attraction was simply the lure of the unplumbed. Because she was new and unknown to him –

The man with the lantern, coming up, touched Frank's arm. "Sorry to cut in but some of the boys over there is beginnin' to talk rope, Frank."

"Rope?" Frank looked at him blankly.

"If you don't want him hoisted you better git over there."

Frank grabbed the lantern and strode into the crowd. Kelly stepped in front of him, barring the way. "We're takin' care of this."

Frank brushed him aside and came through the mob, not daring to believe, and saw the shape on the ground. He brought up the lantern, feeling the breath swell inside him. Luck! He remembered the scream then and looked for blood. He rolled Tularosa over with his foot without finding any. Caught by a hoof maybe, simply knocked out.

"Couple of you gents pick him up and come with me."

Frank heard growls. No one moved. Frank's narrowing eyes saw what he was up against. He set down the lantern. "Pick him up, Kelly."

"Stay outa this, Frank. That bastard's killed five men in this town!"

"That gives you the right to string him up?" Frank looked at them bleakly. "Not while I'm packing tin."

"Kinda feelin' your oats, ain'tcha?" One of Kimberland's outfit pushed up with a hand sliding over the brass of his shell belt. "Go sit in your office if you don't like the play."

"Take him!" somebody yelled from the back, and when Frank twisted his head the whole crowd surged against him. A Church cowhand swung at him, numbing the nerves at the side of Frank's shoulder. Frank rammed the flat of an arm into the fellow, driving him backward. A growl welled out of the mob. Someone fetched Frank a staggering blow on the head. Another tried to climb on his back. Frank shook him off and brought up Church's gun.

"If you want to play rough you'll find out what rough is."

Those nearest Frank backed off a little. He dropped into a crouch, got Tularosa half upright. Frank let the man sag across his left shoulder. He lurched erect, darkly considering the crowd, knowing that when he moved they'd make their try.

"Don't be so damned proud," Kelly growled from the left of him.

Last year Kimberland had lost two riders to Tularosa. Kelly, teamstering for Kimberland, certainly understood the temper of this bunch. There were other Kimberland riders in sight and these were getting set, grimly shifting to box Frank.

It occurred to Frank that Tularosa fully deserved anything these people were able to do to him. But he was a prisoner of the law now, Frank's responsibility, and to turn loose of the man would be to admit he couldn't cope with this. Frank said with the wind away down in his belly, "I'm drilling the first guy that gets in my way," and was about to start into them when hoof sound climbed above the growls coming at him. Wood screamed harshly against the gouge of a wheel rim as the wagon came around in a shrieking half circle driven by the girl straight into the crush of angry men.

There were startled shouts and oaths as the men jumped back to avoid being trampled. One, moving too late, was struck by the wood and knocked over. The vibrations of his frightened cry were lost in the wagon's racket as the girl braced herself against the pull of the wild-eyed horses.

"Hurry!" she called impatiently, shaking the hair back out of her face.

Frank heaved his prisoner into the wagonbed, catching hold of the tailgate as she let the team go. Several guns barked behind them as Frank vaulted up. The girl swung the excited horses past the Chuckwagon's shine and cramped them into a careening run across the trash-littered open between the cook's dutch ovens and Fentriss' livery. Climbing over Tularosa's jouncing shape – the man was trying to get up now – Frank cuffed him down and, ducking the battered brass-cornered trunk, jarred onto the seat beside her. Breathing hard he reached for the lines. The girl wouldn't yield them.

"County seat's Vega, isn't it?" she yelled in his ear.

"We're not heading for Vega!" Frank scowled over a shoulder. "Cut around back of the jail."

"Are you crazy?" She kept the team pointed south and reached for the whip. "That crowd –"

Frank closed his hands on the lines ahead of her hands, sawing the horses around into the east and bringing them back through the

39

grass toward the street again. Fentriss' railed pens came out of the dust and he drove to the right of them, fetching the team up behind the dark jail.

He got the animals stopped and jumped down. "Obliged," he mumbled, hurrying toward the back door. He got the keys from his pocket and pushed the door open. With bent head he stood listening, then came back for Tularosa.

"I suppose," the girl said, "you've got your mind set on a halo. Just watch out you don't wind up with a harp. Some of those fellows –"

"They'll get over it." Frank grabbed Tularosa's feet and pulled. The man was conscious but he certainly wasn't himself by considerable. He was able to stand with Frank hanging onto him. Frank steered him toward the door.

Angry shouts interlarded with hoof sound came from the street where mounted men were milling in cursing confusion. "Wait –" the girl cried – "I'll help you."

"You can do that best by –"

"Maybe I can pull that bunch off your neck."

Frank twisted to look up at her. "Now who's reaching for a harp! You want to get yourself killed?"

40

She untangled the lines. There was the flash of her teeth. "I'm used to risk." She shook out the lines and clucked her tongue at the team. "Ever turned a herd with a lighted match?" With a laugh drifting back to put a catch in Frank's throat, she fingered the horses into a run. Before Frank could say "Damn!" she was whipping them around the back end of the hotel. Past the dark barn of the stage company she put the team at the street, bouncing east on two wheels as she went out of Frank's sight.

The crowd yelled. Riders tore after her, streaking across the mouth of the alley. Frank, swearing, shoved Tularosa ahead of him. He slammed the door and bolted it.

There was a light in the office and a man in the corridor with a gun in his hand.

CHAPTER THREE

Frank, frozenly staring, stood unable to move for the better part of a second, hearing Tularosa stumbling somewhere off to the left of him. Sucking in a long breath he came out of it, following the prisoner, pushing him into one of the cells, yanking the grill shut.

41

He wiped the sweat off his neck and tramped on up the corridor. "A fine thing, peon, rambling around this place with a gun in your hand. You trying to get yourself shot?"

The other fellow laughed. "The gun is yours. I got your horse too. How does it feel, packing the tin in this town?"

Frank took the gun and put it away between belly and trousers. "For eighty a month you got the chance to find out."

"Not me. I'm comfortable –"

"You only think you are." Frank, turning, rummaged in the desk, got his hand on what he wanted and tossed a nickel-plated star at the other. "Pin it on, bucko. You'll find it beats misbranding cattle."

The man rubbed his nose, staring at Frank like he was trying to figure out just how much of that was meant. He was short for this country, heavy-built and dark with a bristling mustache that hid his mouth. He thought and spoke in the manner of a gringo but his name was Chavez and, mostly, folks eyed him with their heads to one side. He said, "You fool! How long would this town stand for *me* on the payroll?"

"My worry," Frank grinned. "Pin it on. I got a chore for you. Danny Settles came in about a half hour ago. I want him found and fetched over here."

Chavez's black stare dug into Frank bitterly.

"Go on, you damn loafer. Pronto."

"That soft streak, gringo, will one day be the end of you."

Frank waved him away and dropped into the chair. He took Will Church's pistol out of his holster. He said, "You find Tularosa's?"

Chavez shook his head. "Old man Wolverton got it." He scowled and licked his lips and shifted his weight from one foot to the other. "Frank, damn it, you don't want –"

"Get going, you sorry peon. We've got to have a jailer and who can we get but Danny without putting up more than the cost of his keep?"

He shook the shells from Church's pistol and only one of them thumped when it hit the desk. He'd been lucky there, too, he thought. He squinted through the dirty barrel, got a rag from the desk and was cleaning it when he heard Chavez leave. He shook his head, unconsciously frowning.

He reckoned there would be a deal of talk about him taking for a deputy a Mexican who two-thirds of them figured to be a rustler. Luck had caught Tularosa for him. He'd put a star on Chavez because he had to have a man no one else could hire away from him, a gun that would stay loyal. It was simple as that. The soft streak the man had charged him with didn't enter into his selection at all. At least Frank hoped he wasn't quite that much of a fool.

They'd all be watching him, weighing his actions, quick to turn to their own advantage any weakness he was careless enough to show. By Frank's observation a marshal's life was a touch-and-go thing, safe only so long as he could keep the whip hand. Gurden's hard malice would be all the time looking for a new crack to stab at; the storekeeper put no trust in him and Arnold would stand behind Frank only so long as it might suit W. T. Kimberland.

Pushing Church's gun aside Frank put his elbows on the desk. Still thinking, he slid them back and rubbed his hands along its edge, feeling less and less satisfied with this shaky damn perch he had got himself onto. If Kimberland was dreaming up a further expansion of Bar 40 range – and there was talk enough to indicate there might be truth in the rumor – Frank could see how the man would want a galoot packing the star who'd be inclined to see his side of things. This had been a bad year with not half enough rain and the syndicate was caught in a falling market with a heap more cattle than they had any grass for. Roundup was less than a week away and if Kimberland couldn't manage to get himself out of the bind he'd have to drive to Dodge and take for good beef considerable less than it had cost to raise. A lot of herds had been ahead of him while he'd sat here fidgeting in the hope of additional rain. There was still grass on these flats but –

A faint scratch of sound pulled Frank's head up. This quick he was cocked to send a hand streaking beltward but he kept the hand still and held the rest of him likewise. Too close to the desk and too late for it anyway. Tularosa's saddlemate – that old jasper he'd disarmed at the blacksmith's – stood just inside the open door.

The old coot had the look of a hungry wolf. He held a gun at his hip and the slanch of his eyes said he'd just as lief use it. "Git him out."

"Keys are in my back pocket," Frank said, looking disgusted.

"Son, I ain't aimin' to tell you twice."

Frank, shrugging, got up. He found it harder than he'd reckoned to turn his back on this ranny but Frank wanted it understood he wasn't about to go off the foolish end of this. With two fingers he fished the ring of keys from his pocket. "Now shuck the gun," Draicup's rider said.

Frank got up and let it fall out of his pants. The sound of its drop held a world of finality.

The old man said, "Git him outa there now."

A pile of thoughts churned through Frank's head and were discarded. He tramped down the echoing corridor with the old trail hand keeping plenty of space between them. No chance to whirl and grab. Too much promise of stopping a bullet.

"That you, Dogie?" Tularosa growled.

The old vinegarroon grunted. "Git that cage open, boy."

It was in Frank's mind that he might still manage to block this. All he needed to do was pitch these keys into one of the cells, into one of those shut and empty ones. Before this sidewinder got things in hand again Chavez ought to be coming into the place with Settles.

But Frank hadn't enough faith in the plan to go through with it. Chavez would walk into this blind and probably get himself shot. And they might drill Frank for spite. Tularosa took hold of the bars. He was grinning.

Three feet short of Tularosa Frank turned. "You –"

"Git that door open quick!"

The old geezer was in one hell of a sweat. It was even money he had watched Chavez leave. *"Don't shoot,"* Frank yelled – *"bend that gun over his head!"*

It was the oldest trick in the deck, but it impelled the man to make a choice at a time he couldn't afford to get tangled up in thinking. Frank flung the keys, saw them whack Dogie full in the kisser. The old fool fired but he was still off balance and before he could trigger again Frank tied into him, smashing him wickedly against iron bars.

Frank grabbed the man's gun wrist, savagely twisting, forcing the muzzle of the weapon away from him. Dogie fought like a wildcat with a panting ferocity that carried Frank back and came within a twist of breaking Frank's hold. The fist that was free slammed into Frank like a jackhammer. A bony knee slashed at Frank's groin. The old man's head nearly tore off Frank's jaw.

He tried again for Frank's groin and this time found it. Frank's whole body felt that knee going through him. He was lost in red fog. But Dogie, swinging the gun at Frank's head, didn't have as much room as he thought he had. The pistol's long barrel clanged against a cell bar, the blow grazed Frank's neck and Frank, staggering into him, bore the old man off his feet. So much violence seemed to have used the man up. Frank, half smothering him, found Dogie's wrist again, cracking it against the floor until the gun fell out of his fingers.

Frank, rolling clear of him, heard the wild grumble of Tularosa's cursing. Frank pushed onto his feet but that damned old ranny wouldn't own to being whipped. With the breath rattling around in him like a windbroken bronc he was after the gun again, talon-spread hand almost onto it when Frank, snarling with outrage, stamped a boot on it, twisting cruelly. Dogie screamed. Frank, with a fistful of shirt, hauled him upright, slamming him back against the iron bars.

The old man looked bushed. The eyes rolled around in his head like loose marbles. Frank could almost feel sorry for him. He propped him up against the cell, holding him there by that fistful of shirtfront and, wondering reluctantly if he ought to call Doc, reached down the limp arm for that boot-bloodied hand.

Frank never did find out what hit him. Through the blinding explosion of pain in his head he had one final instant of full comprehension. The old jasper had possomed, played him for a sucker. Then something exploded in the region of Frank's guts and he swung down a red spiral into the black of oblivion.

CHAPTER FOUR

He came back to the rasp of men's voices. There was a light above him someplace. He had a feeling of motion which abruptly ceased and a bunk's ropes aroused to exquisite torture every misused bone and muscle in his body. Through the swimming red slits of his squeezed-shut gaze he saw Chavez bending over him, muttering and scowling. He saw Chavez twist his head. "Get that sawbones," the Mexican growled.

Frank, shoving up, pushed him out of the way. Pain splintered through him. The breath got stuck in his throat. The room rocked and wavered. He saw Settles' white face and got onto his feet, reeling, swearing. By the feel of his ribs someone had put the boots to him. Anger came into his throat like bile. "Say something, damn you!" he snarled at Chavez.

The Mexican, considering him, said at last, "They got away."

Frank shut his eyes. Already, in his mind, he could hear the avid whispers: *Whipped to a standstill. Licked by a stove-up trail hand.*

Settles shuffled his feet, flapped his hands. "It's my fault, Frank. I'd got through at the store –"

"I know whose fault it is." Frank said bitterly, "How long they been gone?"

Chavez shrugged. "Long enough. Took a while to get you out of there. They shut you into one of them cells, took the keys. We had to saw out the lock."

Well, swearing about it wasn't going to help now. Frank ran a hand gingerly over his ribs and wondered if he should try to locate John Arnold. Settles, watching Frank's hand, asked if Frank was sure he hadn't better have the doctor. Frank squeezed his fists shut. Chavez remarked without giving it any importance. "That woman's waitin' to see you. The one with the wagon."

Frank scowled but fetched his head around. "Where is she? What's she want?"

"Never said. I guess she's outside settin' in it."

Frank got Church's pistol off the desk. He guessed the least he could do was be civil. It certainly wasn't her fault he had let them get the best of him. He told Settles:

"Look around. See if you can turn up

those keys." He sloshed on his hat, telling Chavez to hold the place down.

He saw his horse where Chavez had tied it. He saw the girl. In the light from the windows, as he stepped up to the wagon, he could see she wasn't at all hard on the eyes. Couldn't hold a candle to Honey but she was worth a second look. He asked, "What happened?" and did not think to take off his hat.

"I expect they didn't much like it."

"Didn't bother you, did they?"

Her shoulders moved. She put her hands in her lap. "I hear that fellow got away from you. . . ."

Frank's cheeks got hot. "That's right," he said bitterly. "It'll probably blow over." He didn't really believe that; it just seemed the thing to say. Gurden, for one, would make all he could of an old man getting the best of their marshal. If Gurden could talk Krantz around he'd have the star off Frank's shirt. Frank might try to horse others but he was honest with himself. "They give you any trouble?"

She shook her head. "Of course not." She seemed amused. "I told you I could take care of myself."

Frank expected she really believed that. He took in the blue corduroy skirt, the dark

51

corduroy jacket and small round hat pinned atop her red hair – a kind of chestnut sorrel, he thought – and resentfully found her too cool.

Women had their place in this country and Frank would have been the last to deny it, but this girl was too self-possessed for him. "Well, thanks," he said testily, and was turning away when Church came around the end of her wagon. Frank's mouth turned thin. "I told you, Will, to get out of town."

"I got something to say to you –"

"Say it and get going."

Church showed the umbrage that was smoldering inside him, but he had hold of himself. He looked sober now. "When this town's had enough I'll take care of you, Frank."

"Don't let the badge stop you."

"Never mind. Just remember I gave you warning." Church, wheeling, twisted his head to stare up at the girl. He managed a parched smile, touched his hat and went on.

"Who was that?" the girl asked.

"Will Church." Frank spoke shortly. He was in a poor frame of mind and made no attempt to conceal his irritation. "Will's old man owns six thousand head of cattle."

She smiled. "How many do you own?"

52

Frank growled, "None!" and was turning back toward the office when she said:

"Frank, I wonder if you could...." Her voice trailed off and then came back more determinedly: "I'm trying to find –"

But Frank had closed his mind to everything but Tularosa and the stove-up codger who had whipped him. He went inside.

Chavez with a hip on the edge of the desk looked up, started to speak, looked again and kept silent. Frank dropped into the chair. "You got any ideas?"

"About what?"

"That rustling."

Some of the outfits going up the trail last year had been bothered by stock thieves and the word coming back was that these fellows were getting bolder. Chavez's look showed he understood what was in Frank's mind. His mouth tightened a little but he shook his head. "All that talk was hot air. I had nothing to do with it."

Frank considered him, then said gruffly, "The hell with it. One thing I *don't* have to worry about in this job is cattle." He slipped Church's gun back into his holster. He looked around for his own but guessed Tularosa had got away with it. "What you reckon old Kimberland's up to?"

53

Chavez shrugged elaborately. "I expect," he said finally, "he probably wants to feel he's got the law in his corner."

Frank got up and tramped around. He felt jumpy as a frog. "I think the old pirate's getting ready to grab more range. Plenty of grass up there on the Bench. Enough to see him through for sure. Like to know what he thinks he's bought with this tin."

Chavez nodded. "He aims to get value. But Sam Church is the tight one – he wouldn't give a prairie dog room for a burrow. Hear you slapped Will's horns down."

Frank waved that away. "Danny found those keys yet?"

Chavez shook his head. "Will's eying the Bench, too. If he could grab off that grass they'd be as big or bigger'n Kimberland."

"You think Settles understands we're counting on him for jailer?"

"I told him." Chavez searched Frank's face. "Krantz won't like it."

"Hell with Krantz," Frank growled and, with a wrench of bruised muscles, got a drawer out of the desk and started pawing through it. He shoved it back with a grimace. "Wonder where Joe kept his liniment?"

"What am I supposed to be doing for that fortune the town's paying me?"

54

Frank squeezed a hand against his forehead, twisting his face up. He felt six years older than Moses. "Damn but I got a head! Hell, you can take over at two. Right now, if you don't aim to pound your ear, you can go and help Danny chase down those keys."

Frank stepped into the street.

The girl was gone with her wagon. He was sorry now for the rudeness he had shown her; he was sorry about a lot of things. He slapped the dun with tired affection and wondered how much longer Chip Gurden would be content to let him wear this badge.

It was turning colder. The wind was getting up. There was the feel of winter in it. Frank got his brush jacket off the saddle, shook it out and shrugged into it, swearing a little at the hitch of mauled sinews. He really ought to rub something into them.

He got onto the horse and sat listening a while. There was plenty to hear but the street didn't seem near as noisy as it had. He caught the bawl of a steer and peered off toward the bedgrounds, seeing only solid black beyond the shine of Fentriss' lantern.

That girl, it crossed his mind, may have come from the herd; he didn't, however, put much stock in the notion. Women, as a rule, didn't travel with trail outfits. He didn't want to think of her, didn't want to think about that jail break, either. He hoped Dogie's crushed hand was giving him hell.

The moon was gone, lost in a welter of piled-up clouds. No light at the smithy. The Chuckwagon's owner had given up, too. Must be getting on for twelve. Up the line, in front of the Flag, he saw four-five hombres with their heads together. He didn't hear any singing. Fiddle squeal poured out of the Opal where business was really whooping it up. He heard a woman's high laugh. East, near the bridge, a jerkline freight crawled wearily toward him. These were the bad hours.

Time to move and get into his job. He threw one final look behind and saw two men come out of the pool hall, gab for a moment and head for Gurden's. As they pushed inside Frank saw Kelly behind the batwings. Frank and Kelly had done a lot of helling around together while working for the Churches. Even after Kelly had quit and gone to hauling for Bar 40 they'd continued to see quite a bit of each other whenever, like now, Kelly got to town. These last few months they'd seemed to be drifting away from each other; Kelly'd been spending a lot of his time with one of the floozies who worked for Minnie. Still it was odd, now he

56

stopped to think back on it, he hadn't asked Kelly to be his deputy. Perhaps, without knowing it, the man's connection with Kimberland had decided Frank to pass him up for Chavez. He thought Kelly showed poor judgment loafing around at Gurden's.

Frank pushed it out of his mind and rode east, passing the hotel and gloomily wondering if Honey was spending the night there. She sometimes did on a Saturday night. When her father had business in town she came with him. But he hadn't seen Kimberland, only Bill Grace and some punchers and that Bar 40 wagon that had been pulled up in front of Krantz's store. It wasn't there now. The Mercantile was closed.

Frank saw the barbershop lamp wink out. It was quiet here around the stage depot. Halbertson's hay shed was lost in the shadows. Beyond this, south, there were no lights showing. Continuing east Frank crossed the street's blowing dust in front of the freighter and, rounding Wolverton's Saddlery, cruised into Snob Hollow.

It was the first time Frank had ever ventured this far beyond the limits proscribed by the town for his kind. It gave him a queer turn to be riding here now with the town's approbation. Krantz's house was dark. Frank knew which was which from many travels across the range beyond the river with its fringe of willows. Wolverton's residence, too, was dark, and most of the others. But there were lights behind the lumber king's blinds. Probably throwing a party of some kind.

Prowling the shadows Frank turned back. Putting the dun into the street at a watchful walk he continued to frown as he considered his troubles, reminded of hunger by the yeasty smells coming out of the bake shop where the Swede, with his shirt off, was punching up dough. Nobody showed on the walks east of Gurden's. Frank, smelling coffee, eyed the New York Cafe but he kept the horse moving. He pulled up his collar. That wind was getting some real teeth in it.

Frank reached the Flag. Its crowd had thinned, no longer hiding the bar. He saw Gurden off in a corner talking from the side of his mouth at Old Judge (a drunken sot) who was the only appeal a man had around here without he was willing to drive a hand beltward. At any other time Gurden's presence in the Flag would have caught up Frank's interest, but right then he hardly noticed. Tularosa was on his mind.

He passed Minnie's and, going on to the Trench Brothers' yard, wheeled the dun well away from those black piles of stacked lumber. With the wind blowing through him he passed Minnie's heading back, and was deep in the shadows growing out of that vacant lot when the saddle jarred under him, telegraphing shock the whole length of his body.

The horse flung its head down and had already humped by the time Frank caught the sound of the shot. He had his hands full keeping the animal under him. He spurred the dun around in a crow-hopping circle but there was nothing to see. The bushwhacker was too smart to try his luck again with Frank watching.

Prodded by anger Frank went over to the Flag, remembering Gurden. Frank was about to vault down, go charging in, when a shout came racketing out of the adjoining pool hall. Frank's head whipped around. He forgot about Gurden; what he saw pulled him over to the pool hall.

CHAPTER FIVE

Frank came through the door of the pool hall like the wrath of God. Every face jerked his way except the face of Jace Brackley. Most were startled, some appalled, by the violent passions unleashed in this room; some relief, some resentment at Frank's arrival showed too. Will Church's florid cheeks were still twisted with fury. One white-knuckled fist gripped a cue, butt end out, raised like a club. Blood made a bright splash of color on the knob of it. A second cue lay broken near Brackley on the floor.

"Church," Frank said, "start talking."

"The bastard tried to knock me down!"

No one disputed this. Frank, staring around, jerked his chin at the nearest strange rider. "You boys with that trail herd?" When this was admitted he said to the other one, "You got anything to add?"

The man shook his head and looked like he wished he was someplace else. Frank, sheathing his pistol, stabbed his look back at Church. "Why'd Brackley jump you?"

Young Church said, affronted, "How the hell should I know? Them damn Benchers is apt to do anything." He tossed the bloodied cue away from him and gave Garrison, the hall's proporietor, who was stirring uneasily, a hard look. Garrison quieted. Church wiped his hands against the seams of his trousers and, with a black look at Frank, started to step around him.

"Stand hitched," Frank said. "You're staying right here until Jace comes around."

They were all watching Will, and Church with the weight of that pressure upon him swelled up like a carbuncle. "Who do think you're talkin' to, Carrico?" He drew a half step nearer, dark with outrage. Before he could loose any more of his lip, Brackley rolled over with a groan and sat up. He looked around blearily and put a hand to his head. He eyed the blood on his fingers and, again reaching up, gingerly felt of the ear that had been half torn away. He pushed himself off the floor.

Frank said, "What happened, Brackley?"

The rancher, keeping his eyes on Church, took the hat one of the drovers held out to him. "Nothing I can't take care of," he said, and staggered out of the place without further talk.

Church, cracking a grin, made as though to start after him. Frank put a hand out. "Just a minute."

Will jarred to a stop, the dart of his eyes turning narrowly watchful. "Takin' that tin pretty serious, ain't you?"

Frank kept digging into Will with his stare. Church didn't like it and something shifty in the man began to squirm under so long an inspection. Again he started around

61

Frank and this time Frank let him go. But at the door Will's bile caught up with him and he said, bitterly wheeling, "Give a thirty-a-month cow-walloper a badge to pin on and –"

Frank asked quietly, "You want I should shut that big mouth of yours?"

"Mebbe," Church sneered, "you better look at your hole card. For a jasper that's let a pair of saddle tramps sucker him –"

Something he saw in Frank's stare muzzled the rest of it. With a strangled oath he reached for the door, recoiling when it came suddenly at him. Kimberland's foreman, Bill Grace, came in from the night with a gust of cold air, turning all the way around to stare after the man as Church plunged blindly out through the opening.

"Well!" Grace said, taking a sharp look at Frank, "somebody sure must've shoved a burr under his tail. Ain't seen Will move so fast since the time that centipede crawled up his pants leg."

A couple of cowpunchers laughed. Danny Settles came in with his long coat flapping around him. His unlined face lighted up when he saw Frank. "We found those keys!"

"All right," Frank said, catching the grins. "You get on back," he said curtly. "I'll be over there directly."

He saw Settles' face fall, but the man turned and went out. The two trail hands, racking their cues, also left. One of the others said, dourly critical, "You ain't hired that halfwit fer anythin', hev you?"

"He's acting as jailer," Frank admitted.

Bill Grace said, "The town fool for jailer and a cow-thievin' Mex for deputy. I expect the taxpayers –"

"Any pay Danny rates will come out of my pocket."

"All we need now is some of them Benchers on the Council! I don't wonder that killer got away from you."

"You feel so strong about it," Frank said, "why'n't you go run him down? Maybe they'd make *you* marshal, then your boss could have things just like he wants them." Frank hadn't meant to let go of that last, but the words were out now and he had to stand back of them.

The Bar 40 ramrod looked him up one side and down the other. "It's sure as hell time this town hired a *man* to do its work." With another hard look and a snort he departed.

Chet Garrison dug an elbow into Frank's ribs. "Looks like you been told, boy." There was a vein of friendliness in the man's tone Frank hadn't looked for. A suggestion of that spirit was in some of these other faces. It

63

warmed him, washing away some of his bitterness, allowing him to recover in some measure his sense of proportion. He grinned tiredly and left and outside climbed into his saddle.

The blow was whipping itself into a gale. He had to bend his head against it. Everything seemed to have got itself in motion; dust, trash – even the damned shadows. What few horses were still at the hitchrails had sidled around to get their rumps to the wind. Blinds flapped and banged, but nothing disturbed the wail of the fiddles coming through the doors of the Opal.

It was getting colder than frogs. Frank thrust his hands in his pockets, content to guide the dun with his knees. Then, remembering, he snatched his hands out again. He'd need every advantage a man could get if he bumped into Tularosa.

The dun was breasting the Mercantile, shuttered for the night, when a hunched-forward shape floundered out of the shadows. Frank's instant reaction was to reach for his pistol. Fear of ridicule was greater than Frank's fear of trouble. The man wasn't Tularosa. Believing the fellow was drunk Frank swerved aside but the man cut after him, clutching his hat, and Frank was close enough to recognize Kelly.

"Was figurin'" Kelly shouted, "you might could use a little help."

Frank put the dun into the lee of Ben's Furniture. Kelly, lurching after him, still clutched at his hat. He caught hold of the gelding's cheekstrap.

"Thought you were hauling for Kimberland," Frank said.

Kelly snorted. "Old friends come first."

"I've got Chavez now."

"Wind's swingin' around." Kelly brought the gray blob of his face back to Frank. "Heard about that. Won't be no use to you. Ain't nobody goin' to take orders from no halfbreed."

Frank stared down at him uncomfortably. He was tugged one way by ties of past friendship, dragged another by allegiance to the man he had hired. There was some truth in Kelly's words; Chavez would put some people's backs up. Town Council had ought to be thought about too. Frank could use them both till he got shut of Tularosa. But he could hardly afford to hire Kelly out of pocket.

Seeming almost to read Frank's thoughts the man said, "Hell, I'll work for nothin'. Glad to string along till these damn cows quit comin' through here." He let go of the dun, stepping back like it was settled. Frank said, thinking of Settles, "I can't just kick Chavez out like a dog."

A note of resentment put an edge on Kelly's voice. "Never mind. I ain't quitting a good thing to play second fiddle to no Mex. If I don't rate top spot with you –" He seemed to catch himself then. He made an irritable gesture. "What I mean – Damn it, you got Will Church down on you. Gurden's still riled about that killer gettin' loose. Krantz hates your guts. Now, with this pair of yaps you've latched onto –"

"What you mean," Frank said, "is that I've made a fine hash of this."

"I never said that!"

"You might just as well have. It's the truth."

Kelly stared up at him, hugging his coat, edging back more to get out of the wind. "Hell, you know what this town is! All I was tryin' to say is you've mebbe bit off more than one guy can handle –"

"Hickok's handling Abilene."

"Hickok!" yowled Kelly. "What you need's *help* – a friend at your back, another gun you can count on."

"I ain't heard of Bat Masterson hiring any bodyguard."

66

"You think you can gun-whip this town into line? Talk sense, damn it to hell!"

"Does it make sense for you to quit a soft job to go with a man who's apt to get burnt down before he's two hours older?" Frank picked up his reins. "I've got to get moving."

Kelly followed him, the gale at their backs now. "Swingin' into the southwest – we're like to hev weather." He relapsed into silence, hanging onto Frank's stirrup.

At the Bon Ton Frank wheeled the dun around. Keeping to a pattern was just asking for trouble; Snob Hollow could look after itself for a spell. Coming into the light from the New York Cafe he got hold of Kelly's hand and grimly pushed the man's fingers across the swell of his saddle, across the ripped place where the bullet had struck. Kelly jerked back like he'd touched a snake.

Frank looked down at him with inscrutable eyes. "That leather won't bite. Be thankful, old friend, you ain't called on to help."

The teamster twisted his head against the slap of the wind. They were passing Ben's Furniture before he got enough breath back to make himself heard. "Tularosa?"

Frank shrugged. He seemed to be catching the habit from Chavez. "Him, or another.

Don't make much difference to a stiff whose slug tags it."

They were opposite the jail, hardly ten strides from Gurden's batwings when Kelly pulled up. "Mebbe I better be turnin' off here. I –"

The hammering explosions of two shots, one climbing hard over the heels of the other, barreled through Kelly's words. Both men flung startled looks at the Opal. Frank, sending the dun forward, was out of the saddle on skidding bootheels, catching at a porch post, smashing into the half-leaf doors. Two more shots, slamming the doors, drove him back. He had no further thought for Kelly. He dropped flat to the porch planks, palming his gun, firing beneath the doors at the gangling shape diving through a side window. One of the doors jerked over Frank's head but he was already coming off of the boards, throwing himself headlong at the mouth of the alley.

He was too mad for caution but there was no one in sight when he looked into the alley. The man he had fired at was Tularosa and now, still staring, Frank found himself shaking as caution belatedly sank its hooks into him. He backed away from that slot and swiveled a look round for Kelly. The teamster wasn't in sight. *Gone up the other side,* Frank thought, and ran along the dark front of the Mercantile, feverishly pushing fresh loads into the cylinder.

At the entrance to the passage between Krantz's and Ben's Furniture he fell back a moment, listening, but the racket of the wind made hearing other sounds unlikely. He ran east as far as the barber's pole. Dropping into a walk, he moved up that dark alley. This blackness had an almost tangible quality, folding around him like the wrap of a blanket, cutting off the wind, reducing its clamor to a kind of muffled groan.

He stopped three paces from the passage's end but still heard nothing he could imagine was Tularosa. Frank knew the chance he would take if he looked. A cold sweat filmed his flesh as he moved into the open but no bullet came at him. In this moonless murk the killer could have crouched ten feet away without discovery.

Frank wanted to turn back but the words of Kimberland's foreman still rankled. He raked the dark with angry eyes, weighing his chances and not at all liking them. Frank, jaws clenched, moved forward, driven by the knowledge of his responsibility. If Frank had kept hold of Tularosa the man wouldn't be here now.

Several times Frank stumbled in the trash

69

underfoot and twice his boots sent tin cans rattling but he reached the back of the Opal without having discovered any trace of his quarry.

Swearing under his breath, he went around to the front, pausing on Gurden's porch for another look at those swing doors. Then he stepped in and talk broke. He tramped down an opening lane and found Brackley. The man was dead. Frank's eyes stabbed Gurden. "Let's have it."

"Brackley come in here maybe half an hour ago. Said he wanted to talk so we went in the back room." Gurden's eyes were bland. "Turned out he wanted a loan."

Frank had been wondering what had fetched Brackley in. The man hadn't liked towns, hadn't been to South fork more than twice in three years. "So you gave it to him. Backed, of course, by a plaster on his spread."

Gurden's mouth thinned around its tightened grip on his cigar. "Naturally."

"Got it handy?"

"It's in the safe."

"So you gave him the money and put the lien in your safe. Then the pair of you came out – and Tularosa shot him."

Gurden's eyes were bland no longer. They gleamed like bits of metal and there was color creeping into his beefy jowls. "I didn't see the man killed; I was still in my office when I heard the shots."

Frank discovered Wolverton in the crowd and tipped his head at him. "You want to say anything?"

The saddle merchant said, without looking at Gurden, "Jace came out by himself."

"And where was Tularosa?"

Wolverton shrugged. "I didn't see him."

Anger came into Frank's face then. "Did *anybody* see him?"

A Boxed T man said, "He came in by that door over there," and pointed across the room toward the gun shop. "He slid in just as Brackley came out of Chip's office. He yelled 'Brackley!' and when Jace turned, shot him."

A Kimberland rider said, "No argument or nothin'." And Bernie, who was by the bar, said, "Tularosa let go soon as he spotted Brackley – just yelled and shot while Brackley was still turning."

"Then jumped for the window, eh?"

"Close enough," Wolverton said. "there was a racket of hoofs and someone come onto the porch. That's when he went for the window."

"All right." Frank looked at Gurden. Then his glance singled out two punchers,

71

Squatting O hands from farther unpriver. "Pack Brackley over to where they've got Jo Ashenfeldt and hang around till I get there." His eyes snapped back to Gurden. "Close up."

In this town Chip Gurden was one-third of the law and he was not in the habit of taking orders from anyone. His reaction was instant. "Now look –"

Frank cut him off. "Take it up with Krantz or Arnold. I want this crowd out of here in three minutes."

Gurden's look swelled with hate. "If you think –"

"Clear this place," Frank said, "or I'll do it." He felt the man's fury swirling round him like a fog, but in the end Chip threw a hand up and his housemen got the exodus started. One of his aprons climbed up on the bar and started putting out lamps. Frank nodded at the Squatting O punchers and they picked Brackley up and joined the departing customers.

When the most of them were out Frank said to the Opal's proprietor, "We'll go into your office and you can show me that lien."

"Go to hell!" Gurden snarled and went into the back room, slamming the door.

Frank was minded to follow but Chavez came in with a double-barreled shotgun.

72

Frank sent him after the furniture man, who was all the coroner they had in these parts. Frank had cooled some by then and decided to shelve the matter of Brackley's plaster until he could secure reliable opinions on the signature.

Leaving the place, he went back to the street and got onto the dun and sat a while, frowning. Then he picked up his reins and rode over to Ben Holliday's furniture place. There was a light at the back, and he got down and went in. Brackley was stretched out alongside Joe's body but the pair who had fetched him were nowhere in sight.

Back at Chip Gurden's the new bouncer, Mousetrap, stepped into the office and carefully shut the bar door. Gurden, eyeing the man bleakly, hauled a bottle off his desk and helped himself to a snort. He was putting it down when somebody's knuckles rattled against the back door. Mousetrap raised the hairy black of his eyebrows and, at Gurden's nod, went across to open it.

Kelly slipped in, twistedly grinning at the sight of the derringer disappearing up Chip's sleeve. "I warned you he was tough."

Mousetrap said, "I kin handle that feller."

"Why didn't you do it when he was growlin' over Brackley?"

Gurden said, "Shut up – both of you." He nodded at the whisky. Mousetrap passed and Kelly, eying the man derisively, caught up the bottle and lowered its level by a third. He set it down, smacking his mouth. Gurden said, "You tried for him yet?"

"Thought you was payin' to get that took care of."

"Where *is* that damn Tularosa?"

"Ain't nobody payin' me to keep cases."

"You know what I told you –"

"Give Tularosa a chance," Kelly grumbled. "He sure as hell took care of Brackley.

Gurden brushed that aside. "I want Frank put out of the way, and I got no time to waste foolin' around, either. You get after him, Kelly. Right away. Tonight."

"I already made one try," Kelly said. "It didn't come off. I hit his damn saddle."

Gurden fished a fresh stogie from his flower-embroidered vest. "What's the matter? You get buck fever? You got the best chance of anyone. You could walk right up and ram a gun in his –"

"That's what you think. I was around when a guy tried that on him once –"

"But you're his *friend*. Damn it, Kelly!"

"If he thinks so much of me howcome I

ain't his deppity? I done everything but git right down on my knees."

"You think he suspects you?"

The teamster said uncomfortably, "How the hell could he?" but there was sweat on his lip.

Gurden struck a match and tipped it under his cigar. Through the smoke coming out of his mouth, he said, "You ain't handled it right. I'll think up a way." He put more smoke around him, rolling the stogie back and forth across his mouth. "Anything'll come out right if a man will put his mind to it." A contemplative look came into his winkless stare and he said in a kind of half drawl, "Wonder what made young Church jump Brackley?"

"He's tryin'," Kelly said, "to steal a march on Kimberland. He's had it in for W. T. ever since the old man told him to keep away from that girl."

"Kimberland told Will to stay away from Honey?"

"I thought you'd heard that." Kelly grinned. "He said things to Will, the way I got it, no man could take off anyone." His grin broadened. "Will thinks the old man needs that grass."

Gurden didn't care what Will thought, or Kelly either. As a matter of fact, he had

75

himself put Will up to bracing Brackley and Brackley, suspecting as much, had come here tonight to tax Gurden with it and to warn him off. Gurden wasn't about to reveal the real truth of it; what had happened to Brackley was pretty near as good as stumbling onto a gold mine. Gurden knew that Kimberland wasn't worrying about his cows. All these feints he was making was to cover up that railroad. Kimberland wanted that Bench for the right-of-way it would give him.

"Well," Gurden growled, changing the subject, "you keep away from Frank. Get hold of Tularosa and send him over here right away. Soon's you've done that, get a note to Frank. Don't talk to him. Get a note to him and tell him you've got to see him in front of the bake shop tomorrow at noon."

This last was spoken so low that Mouse-trap, ten feet away, did not catch it. But Kelly heard. The bristles of hair along the edge of his collar stood straight up at the back of his neck. What Gurden, in effect, was asking him to do was to set Frank up where Tularosa could put a slug in him. The saloonman got up and took Kelly's arm and steered him over to the back door. "Remember –" Gurden's breath on Kelly's

76

cheek was like the kiss of death – "no mistakes this time, eh?"

With the door closed behind him and silently rebolted, Chip Gurden turned, gold teeth glinting, and winked at the curious look Mousetrap gave him. He took off his boots and, carrying them, cut over to the door they'd come through from the bar. With no warning at all Gurden yanked it open.

A man spilled in stumbling out of a crouch as the light broke across him. Turning loose of the boots, Gurden caught the thin shape of his piano player by the front of his shirt and slammed the man bodily into the wall. The fellow cringed from Gurden's look, cheeks ludicrous with fright. "I – I was just comin' in to –"

"You're in now!" Gurden grinned. He flung the whimpering wretch at Mousetrap. "Take care of this joker." He stamped into his boots and stalked through the dark bar. The big clock above it said ten after two.

CHAPTER SIX

Kimberland, unknown to Frank or Arnold, was in town that night, having driven in late with Honey and gone directly to his suite at the Hays Hotel. The girl had gone to bed, worn out. In the dark of his second-floor-front room W. T., still dressed, was very much awake. He was doing what he'd come to do, keeping track of his latest investments.

He knew something of Frank – a lot more than Frank reckoned – but all he knew about Tularosa was that the man rode for Draicup and was a dyed-in-the-wool killer whose guns could be bought. It went against Kimberland's grain to have to deal with such trash but in this case, not caring to be involved, he had no choice. It was imperative that Brackley be got rid of at once. W. T. had learned from one of the man's riders that Brackley would be in South Fork tonight. At considerable inconvenience Kimberland had made his arrangements, knowing something had to be done before this thing got out of hand. He had had two weeks to plan and had the deal pinned down letter perfect, but

78

he couldn't sit back and let events take their course. His entire fortune was at stake, and the way things had recently been going he had to be where he could step in and take a hand if that damned hired killer didn't get the job done.

He'd had a session right away with Bill Grace and bitterly discovered what had happened to Tularosa when he'd been after that girl. But Tularosa had got free, been turned loose on the town again, and Frank apparently hadn't yet caught up with him when Kimberland had heard the guns pound over at Gurden's and seen the two punchers lugging Brackley away. So that part of it was settled.

Stepping back from the curtained window Kimberland yawned and stretched contentedly. It was too bad about Brackley but a man had to look out for himself in this world and he had given the fool an out by offering to buy the damned spread. Brackley had no one to blame but his own bull-headedness. That road represented progress and no one had the right to stand in the way of a country's development. He guessed the rest of those Benchers would understand that now. And before anyone got wise to what was brewing he, W. T. would have that right-of-way in his pocket.

This was why he wanted the Bench, not for the grass – though he could use that, too. But the road came first, that was where his money was. When the Company got their preliminary report, a survey crew would be sent into the region and the value of land would go up like Apache smoke. Which was why he'd held back his beef so long, not for the rain but for how it would look to the rest of this country when Bar 40 scrapped boundaries and moved onto the Bench.

That high shelf would be the obvious choice of any survey. There was no other practical place for a roadbed. It wasn't only that he had to protect his investment; that Bench ran for twenty miles through this country and control of it would net a handsome profit to the man who could deliver it. Tomorrow Bar 40 would start moving cattle.

He heard the creak of the stairs and, guessing this would be Bill Grace again, went over and quietly opened the hall door. His foreman slipped in, and said as soon as the door was shut: "Gurden's bought into this!"

Kimberland grinned. "Joke – ha ha."

"It's no joke," Grace said.

"How could he buy in when he don't even know –"

"He knows, all right. First thing your star-packer done when he went over there was ask what Brackley was doin' in Chip's place. Gurden wiped off his mouth an' said he'd come for a loan which he had made him – *secured by a lien against Brackley's stock and range.*"

"Son of a bitch!"

"The point," Grace said, "is what do we do about it? I told you when we took over Chip's ranch that feller was goin' to lay for you. You better let me shoot him."

If it was just Gurden, Kimberland reflected, it might be better to let him get away with this. But it wasn't just Gurden. Bar 40, on the climb, had tramped roughshod over everyone. The slightest evidence of weakness would bring the whole bunch swarming, and Gurden wouldn't quit with this. He had too long a memory.

"I've got to think," Kimberland said.

"You better think fast if we're pushin' those cattle over there in the morning."

"How did Frank take it? I mean about Brackley's killing and that plaster of Gurden's."

"Acted damn suspicious."

"Good," Kimberland nodded. "Now has Chip really got a lien?"

"He'll damn well produce one –"

"Keep your voice down," Kimberland

grumbled. "We don't want my girl getting up to come in here."

"She wouldn't know a jughandle from a tomato can," Grace said. "All she's got any time for is –" He let go of that line when he caught Kimberland's look. Abruptly then they were both standing tense, faces whipped toward the window. There was a far sound of shots, a sullen rumble like thunder with a shout lifting through it, thinly soaring, suddenly gone. The racket, as Kimberland threw up the window, could mean but one thing to any listening cowman.

"By God," Grace cried, "it's that trail herd!"

Louder, nearer, laced with the terrified bawling of cattle, that trampling roar was like the sound of an avalanche. Cries flew out of the street. The hall door burst open. *"Father!"* A girl with a quilted wrapper clutched about her ran barefooted past the scowling red-cheeked foreman, the loose mass of her hair tumbling about slim shoulders like a cascade of gold in the light from the street. "Father –?" More guns went off and there were yells from below. Bill Grace, swearing, dashed for the stairs.

Kimberland, still at the window, dropped a comforting arm about the girl's shoulder.

The tautness of strain was in his muscles, too.

Honey said, "I'm afraid –"

His watch said 2:30. He allowed her to coax him as far as the rocker. "We're as safe right here as we'd probably be anywhere." He took the girl's hand. "Tonight we've got a new marshal, Sugar. I think you could turn his head very easily."

There was no change in the lovely face but her voice was compliant. "Would that help you, Father?"

"I suppose," he said with just the right inflection, "a woman might find that young scamp attractive."

"Do I know him, Father?"

He smiled down at her quizzically. "He's the fellow who saved you from Church's bull that time." He spoke as to a child. "Perhaps you'd enjoy having lunch with him tomorrow. Of course," he added doubtfully, "Frank's pretty much of a roughneck."

"I could do that," Honey said.

"Town's growing up. Never does any harm to be well thought of by a marshal. Sort of like to have him get the idea us folks from Bar Forty.... Look, just act natural, Sugar. Friendly. That's all I want you to do."

Frank, at the marshal's office, had turned in at two. Danny was tipped back in one of the chairs against the wall, snoring with his mouth opening and shutting with each breath. Frank had left Chavez in charge of the town. Sleep wouldn't come to Frank what with all the banging and clatter being stirred up by that gale. His thoughts were like horses; every fourth or fifth jump they'd take him back to those bodies in the rear of Ben's store. Chavez had shown up with Ben, and the furniture-selling coroner had officially pronounced Brackley dead. Frank had then assembled the contents of his pocket which had included a dog-eared wallet. This last, upon inspection, had proved to contain a handful of silver and thirty-four dollars in hard-used bills. Frank had stared at these blankly.

"What's the matter?" Ben had asked, and Frank had explained about the loan Gurden claimed to have made Jace. Chavez had looked frankly skeptical. Ben had asked, "What about those fellers that carried him over here?"

Frank shook his head and, figuratively speaking, was still shaking it. The men who had brought Brackley here might have taken the money if Brackley'd had it on him but Frank couldn't dredge any confidence from the notion. If a man made up his mind to robbery, where was the sense in leaving part of the haul? It would all have been in Brackley's wallet if he'd had it. Yet Frank had no doubt if he was made to, Gurden would produce a signed lien on Brackley's ranch. There was only one question about this in Frank's mind: Had Gurden had such a paper *before* Brackley's killing?

But this question bred another. Had Gurden arranged Brackley's death or had somebody else? He could foresee the kind of rumors that were no doubt already flying – that would certainly fly if Bar 40 put cattle on Brackley's range. Kimberland or Gurden – which one of them had hired this?

Chavez had put up Frank's dun or he might have gone on the prowl again. He needed sleep. This had been a hard night, about the hardest one he had ever put in. He got up, pulled his boots on, and walked over to the door. Danny was still snoring. Frank stood there a moment, thinking, then went back, got his hat and shrugged into his brush jacket.

He pulled open the door. The suck of the wind put the lamp flame out. Frank heard the shots then, the distant yell, the rumble that followed it. Swearing in the testiness of temper, he ran over to the wall rack and jerked down a rifle. Pausing only to make sure it would take the shells in his belt, Frank hurried into the street.

The night was wild with wind and tumult. The pounding rush of crazed cattle was like the roar of a giant falls. They were nearer now, coming fast, straight for town. He remembered with a sense of bleak irony telling Chavez that cows were the one thing he didn't have to worry about. Looking around, Frank could see there were plenty of others coming out just as he was, armed to do battle for the town's preservation. He caught faintly the excited whickering of horses where a dozen were still uneasily huddling in the grip of tied reins at the rack before the Flag. Why the hell didn't some of those fools climb on them!

The wind flapped his clothes, staggering him with its violence. Digging chin into his collar, he tried to beat his way against it, needing to get into the lee of something, knowing the danger of being trapped in the open. Already those fellows across the way had got under cover. Grit stung his eyes. Dust boiled up by the running herd got so thick he couldn't see ten yards in front of him.

He locked his teeth against their chatter, trying to find Fentriss' barn. To move at all was like bucking a blizzard. Above the racket of hoofs, the shots and the bawling, Frank caught the screech of rending wood, the yells and crash as a building toppled. Those steers wouldn't leave enough of this town for kindling.

He found a wall and stumbled along it, drunkenly reeling, cursing floundering feet that wouldn't track. He could almost feel the snorting breath of those beasts as the leaders funneled into the far end of the street, bawling, horns clacking. The gunshots sounded like cork stoppers popping. Frank reached the end of the wall and the wind hit him solidly, driving the breath back into him. The dust-laden gusts tore at him, half blinding him. He staggered through the stable's door hole into a blackness impenetrable as lamp soot. Loose boards shook and rattled. The place was noisy with the clamor of frightened horses. Frank wiped his streaming eyes on the back of an abrasive wrist.

Across the street through the blowing dust there were patterns of foggy radiance where turned-up lamps shone through the windows, but these didn't make seeing any easier to speak of. The dust cleared a little as the gusts slid into a lull. The herd had been stopped, was beginning very slowly to revolve on itself; but Frank knew, without riders, how chancey was this respite, how swiftly those steers would run again should something upset them. He took his chance while he had it and darted into the open, thinking to get up on the roof of the Mercantile where he'd be able to see a little better.

In the dust and confusion he miscalculated someway and wound up before the half-leaf doors of the Opal. He shouted for Gurden but got no answer. The stopped cattle were still milling in front of Minnie's. He heard Chavez's voice:

"Douse them lamps before you burn up this town! Pronto!"

This seemed to make sense to quite a number of folks. One by one the nearer lights winked out. The horses tied in front of the Flag had gone away with their hitchrail. Gurden hadn't locked up; Frank saw the batwings flap as wind picked up the dust again with a howl. Something flapped, too, behind the herd. Frank felt the ground quiver under him as every steer in it suddenly churned into motion. Frank dived for the Opal.

He knew where the lamps were. He got one, letting go of the rifle, and dragged a match across the seat of his pants. A lantern would have been better, but he took what he could get. His fastest wasn't any too quick. There they came, boiling out of the dust with their eyes big as wash tubs. As Frank crossed the porch and ran into the street some woman cried shrilly, *"Is he crazy?"* And then the herd was engulfing the street like a monster, so near he could see their slobber-flecked chests and the sharp wicked glint of their tossing horns.

Frank flung the flaring lamp high above them.

The herd broke like splatter, the whole front melting away, panicked by the sight of that flame diving at them. Several steers crashed head-on into buildings, adding their terrified bellows to the uproar, but the great bulk of the mass veered off south after the lead steer who, by the kindness of God, took for the largest chunk of open space in sight, trailed by his followers in a curve that tipped east back of Fentriss' livery. One crazed brute, lone-wolfing it up the street through the dust, almost ran Frank down while he was standing there shaking. He fired twice pointblank with his pistol, yet blind panic or momentum carried the animal the length of the Mercantile's front before collapsing.

Frank's legs folded under him. Cramps ravaged his stomach.

CHAPTER SEVEN

Dragging a hand across his mouth Frank shoved up off his knees and got out of the street. There was much random shouting, lights were commencing to flare up behind windows as anxious merchants and the incurably curious came forth out of hiding to assess the damage. The wind – after the manner of that rail and those horses – seemed to have gone somewhere else. Frank could hear occasional gunshots but these were scattered, sporadic, probably mercy slugs for cripples. He supposed he ought to get back to the office where he could be found, but that plaster of Gurden's was still on his mind and he went down Krantz's wagon pass and thumped on the Opal's back door with his fist. He kept at it a long while before convinced he would not get any answer.

He dragged himself around to the front, unutterably weary, almost out on his feet. He guessed he ought to be hunting Tularosa but he just wasn't up to it. He went back to the office and, finding Danny Settles in the bunk, collapsed on the floor.

He woke up in the bunk with the morning sun nearly three hours high. He was so crammed with aches when he tried to move he didn't much care if he never got up. He heard steps outside and Danny Settles came in with his breakfast, his old-young face looking cheerful as a man who has just been handed a king full on aces. "Good morning, Frank."

Frank said contentiously, "Is it?" and grimaced.

Danny, chuckling out of the wealth of his good humor, put the tray down on the desk. Frank sat up. The sight of food nauseated him. "Better eat that yourself." He lay back and stretched out his legs. "Well?" he growled when he discovered Danny watching him.

"It probably doesn't amount to anything," Danny said, "but that pianist at the Opal – Sleight-of-Hand Willie – was over here before daylight. He looked pretty banged up –"

"What'd he want?" Frank asked, showing interest.

"He seemed to think you ought to know Kelly's into some deal with Gurden. Seemed to have the idea that gun –" He broke off as someone pounded the door.

"Come in," Frank said impatiently.

91

It was Councilman Krantz, the Mercantile's owner. His eyes looked like they would jump through his glasses. "That pizness last night –" He shook his head. "I haff mizchudged you, my poy. But you vant to look out for that Chip, he iss after you. He vas ofer to mine house pefore breakfast yet. He vants to take that star avay from you – says you von't enforce that new gun law."

"He was never more wrong in his life," Frank growled. He flung off the blanket and stamped into his boots. He'd lost his hat last night in the wind and reached for Danny's. He said, glowering at Krantz, "Do I look like the kind that would sell a man out!" and caught up his shell belt, slapping it around him.

Danny Settles, alarmed, said, "Frank, where are you off to?"

Even Krantz looked worried. But Frank had had about enough of Chip Gurden. "I'm going to do something I should of done last night!" he said hotly.

He tramped across to the hotel, went up to the barber's room and talked Pete into shaving him at the point of a pistol.

"But gol darn it, man, this is *Sunday!*" Pete protested.

"If you want to see Monday," Frank said, "get busy."

He felt more himself as he went down the stairs. He'd cooled off a little, too, and decided he might as well stop for a cup of coffee, secretly hoping he might catch sight of Honey. He had the dining room to himself except for Joe Wolverton who owned the saddle shop and, not being married, was enjoying a leisurely breakfast. Sight of Joe eating suddenly whipped up Frank's appetite. "Ham and eggs," he told the hasher. "Wreck 'em and fetch the java right away."

He was midway through this food when the swish of a skirt and the tap of high heels swung his face around. A warm pleasure rushed through him when he saw Honey moving between tables. He looked – as the saddle man later told his cronies – "like a winter-starved dogie catchin' a whiff of fresh alfalfa."

It was the first time Frank had got near enough to speak since he had saved her from Church's bull. She completely took his breath away but at least he had sense enough to drag off his hat.

"How are you, Frank?" She came right up to him and put out her hand. She saw the star on his shirt. "So you're our new marshal. Frank, I'm proud of you."

He felt her hand squirm and finally let go

of it. Fussed up and grinning, he stood twisting his hat. She'd filled out a lot, he thought – looked prettier than a basket of chips. Honey, squeezing his arm, laughed up at him softly.

Somebody scraped back a chair and Frank, recollecting Wolverton, became self-conscious and awkward, knowing the man would be taking this in.

Honey, still hanging onto him said, "I think – I'm almost sure – I will be staying over tonight. Abbie's been making some new hats for me. Perhaps we could get together for dinner...."

Frank stared and gulped, his grin showed embarrassment. Then remembering his job he said glumly, "I'll be on duty tonight." But he wasn't on duty this noon – he wouldn't go on before one. He said, brightening, "Could I take you this noon?"

Honey, hesitating, smiled. "That will be all right."

"Swell!" Frank said, forgetting Joe Wolverton, and the waitress who was also watching them with an interest not untinged by envy. "Twelve o'clock?"

Honey took a deep breath. "We'd better make it twelve-thirty. I might not be through by twelve."

Giving his arm a final squeeze, she moved

off toward a table by the windows where the hasher, stiffly smiling, was holding a chair out. She had been nourishing a hope of catching Frank for herself.

The marshal saw Wolverton drop some change on his table and then he noticed Gurden by the cigar case lighting a stogie. Gurden, completely ignoring Frank, was taking Honey apart with his stare. Frank was starting to shove up with his face black as thunder when Kimberland turned into the room from the lobby.

The boss of Bar 40, pulling off his gloves, said: "Hello, Chip – Frank, how are you?" even nodding to Wolverton as he stopped by Frank's table. A cropped black beard concealed the most of his expression. His shrewd eyes probed Frank's and he said with approval, "I think, from what I hear, you must have established some kind of a record last night, stopping that herd with a lamp singlehanded. South Fork certainly owes you a large vote of thanks."

With another brisk nod he went over to Honey. Frank stared after him like a man in a dream. Wolverton, coming up, said, "Nice going, Marshal," and clapped Frank on the shoulder.

Frank finished his meal in a kind of a daze. He probably didn't taste one thing he put into him. He got up when he'd finished and left a silver dollar beside his plate. He was halfway back to the office before, with a scowl, he remembered Chip Gurden. He shrugged and crossed over, intending to wait at the Opal; then he saw Abbie Burks.

She owned the Bon Ton Millinery and, according to the way Frank had got it, was the orphaned niece of rancher John Arnold. She was in her middle twenties and was not a bad looker. The trouble with Abbie, Frank had always imagined, was that she couldn't get over her New England raising. She probably wanted a man bad as any woman, he reckoned, but those she could catch she held off with her stiffness and those she'd have taken wanted something more cozy to warm their beds of a night. Frank had watched her at dances – had even swung her himself, but it had been like hauling around a becorseted flapjack. She hadn't spoke ten words the whole time he had hold of her. When the fiddles had quit Frank had said, "Thanks – Prudence," and gone off and got plastered.

But she seemed glad to see him this morning, actually breaking out a smile, though he could see it was quite a strain. When she held out a hand Frank perversely grabbed and pumped it like she was leaving

96

him her will. Her cheeks got pink and flustered. "My –" she said as if she'd just run a mile, "you certainly gave this town something to talk about! I – I do wish you well, Frank. Uncle John was saying –"

"He still around town?"

"I – why, yes – I think so."

Now what the hell would she blush about that for? She said, her lips pale, "Please let go of my hand, Frank."

"Hell, I washed this morning – took a bath in the hotel."

Anger brightened her eyes and she twisted away from him. "You don't under-stand – you don't even try!" And then her voice broke. "You don't know what it's like to –"

"Abbie," he said, "don't work so damn hard at it."

An indescribable look came over her face and without another word she hurried off toward her shop.

Frank rubbed his jaw. "Women!" he said, and cut back toward the jail. Then he remembered the ride he'd got mapped out to take and went along to the livery. While he was saddling his dun the owner, Fentriss, came up. Frank twisted his head. "You seen Arnold this morning?"

"Nope," Fentriss said. "Ain't seen hide

nor hair of him. Lost John, hev you? Chip can't find his piano pounder, either."

Frank led the dun out and climbed into the saddle. Then he remembered the rifle he had left in the Opal, and rode back to the hotel and got down and went in. The rifle, of course, was only Frank's excuse for another look at Honey, but she and her Dad had already left. He spotted Gurden paring his nails at a table with two others who had just started eating. One was Ben Holliday (coffins and furniture); the other was McFell who owned the Blue Flag. Gurden said, grinning, "McFell thinks your gun law ain't got enough teeth in it."

"I'll put the teeth in it," Frank said, "never worry." He put his eyes on Chip grimly. "I left a rifle in your place."

"Yeah. It's back of the bar. You aim to pay for that lamp?"

Frank tossed two coins on the table, lips twisting. "Where was you when I came back a while later?"

"Pounding my ear, I guess."

"You must sleep like the dead."

Gurden smiled thinly. "I sleep all right." He rolled the cigar across his teeth. "Now why don't you ask me what my place was doing open?"

"Suppose you tell me."

"Well, it seems like I had some company. Somebody tried to get into my safe. When are you going to start earning your money?"

"I suppose," Frank said, "he went off with that paper."

"That's exactly what he did." Gurden's winkless eyes mocked him. "But, being's I had a witness to the deal, I don't look for any trouble when it comes to taking over."

"You didn't say anything about a witness last night."

"Last night I had Brackley's signature. Remember?"

Frank leaned across the table, glance truculent. "You don't give a damn for the truth, do you, Gurden?"

"Oh, it's true enough," Chip said. "Go and look at the safe. You prob'ly scared him away when you come after that lamp. About all I can figure he got off with is five hundred dollar bills and Jace's paper. When I went in there about an hour ago I found this on the floor." He pulled a wadded-up square of cloth out of his pocket.

Frank shook the thing out and felt his stomach turn over. It was a neckscarf, pale blue, with a design of yellow horseshoes. Frank had seen it last night around the throat of Tularosa.

Chavez, as Frank swung into the saddle,

cut across from the gun shop still carrying his shotgun. "What's new with Boss Gurden?"

Frank's stare swept the storefronts. He told Chavez what he had just learned from Gurden and showed him the scarf. "It's his wipe," Frank said bitterly.

The Mexican shrugged. "Chip might of picked that up anyplace." He twisted together a brown-paper cigarette. "He was out of this town about half the night. He rode in about five an' left his bronc back of Minnie's. Make sense to you?"

"Horse over there now?"

Chavez shook his head. "That Mousetrap jigger come an' got it about seven. Rubbed it off well as he could an' told Fentriss he'd had it out for a gallop. I seen that caballo before this guy got to work an' I'm tellin' you it was rode hard."

The most of Frank's attention was still prowling the street, digging into alley mouths, probing black door holes. He couldn't find one hostile sign but the threat of Tularosa, like a wildness, was all about him.

He wiped a dampness away from his lip and picked up his reins and told Chavez, "You keep your eyes peeled. I'm figuring to take a pasear out to Brackley's."

Chavez, staring over Frank's shoulder, said, "Hasta luego. He goin' with you?"

Frank, twisting, saw Kimberland on a powerful looking bay jogging leisurely toward the west end of town. With a growl he spurred after him, discovering another rider angling in at a lope. Frank overtook Kimberland at the edge of the lumber yard. W. T. nodded, pulled off his right glove and, fishing a pair of cigars from his shirt, passed one over. Frank bit the end off and accepted a light from Kimberland's match.

The other rider came up, a grizzled looking man in dust-grimed range gear and, setting back his horse, inspected them like a cat with a knot in its tail. "Who's goin' to pay for all them shot cattle?"

"Take it easy," Frank said. "You ain't the only one hurt."

"I'll sue this damn town!" the man shouted. Frank remembered him then as one of the chair-warmers he'd encountered at Minnie's. Gourd and Vine had lost a lot of stock, crippled and scattered, and you couldn't much blame him for sounding a mite ringy.

Frank said, "You one of the owners?"

"Lassiter. Trail boss. I'll spread the name of this –"

"Friend," Kimberland said, teeth champing his cigar, "let's take a more charitable look at this deal."

Frank, backing him up, said, "Your herd tore down a couple of business establishments and might have leveled the whole town if we hadn't got them turned. We didn't order that wind nor –"

"Wind!" The man spat. "Them steers was spooked deliberate!" He shook a fist in Frank's face. "Somebody's goin' to pay fer it!"

"If you'd kept your crew –"

"Don't give me that! I seen what happened. A bunch of guys come out of the dark flappin' slickers. Draicup warned me what this country was like. You cigar-smokin' bastards think all you got to do is scatter these drives an' after they've gone you kin pick up the pieces!"

Frank said, "That's pretty strong talk."

"This geezer," Lassiter said, "looks like that sonofabitch Kimberland I been hearin' about. Draicup tol' me if I got in trouble to yell. Man, they're goin' to hear me clean back to Corpus!" He spun his horse, glaring furiously, raked its flanks with the steel and tore off toward his camp.

Kimberland said, "He'll cool. Draicup *could* be hitting these herds himself; he's never too far when the cows start to run. But

I don't think it's him. I think Gurden's back of it. Chip and maybe –" He eyed Frank inscrutably. "Here's where I turn off. If you're heading for Brackley's –" He let that go, too. "Frank, you're doing allright. Don't let nobody spook you."

The sun was beginning really to bear down when Frank sighted Brackley's buildings. He wasn't surprised to see the wrinkle of smoke coming out of a stovepipe. The man had employed two riders on a year-round basis. Frank *was* surprised though when, in answer to his hail, the girl of the wagon stepped out of the house.

There were glints of burnished firelight in her hair. Frank was discovering what a girl with curves and a too direct look could do to a man. She had a rifle in her hands but when she saw who it was she leaned it against the weather-grayed wall and a gleam of interest came into her look. Her mouth curved into a slow smile. "Well!" She smoothed the skirt about her thighs and poked a hand at her hair. "You didn't lose much time getting onto my trail."

"What you doing here?" Frank asked suspiciously.

She said after a moment, "I could ask you the same. This ranch isn't a part of your bailiwick."

She wore a thin cotton print that displayed her figure with an almost insolent boldness. Her feet were bare but Frank was trying hard not to notice them. As though perceiving his discomfiture and divining the cause of it she laughed in a way that made his cheeks burn. "I'd of freshed up a little if I'd guessed you were coming."

"Where's the hands?" Frank asked, peering around from his saddle.

With that mop of red hair tumbled about her head she was still coolly watching when Frank pulled his glance back. "Seems they woke up to important business elsewhere when they found I was aimin' to stay on here."

Frank's jaw dropped. The unbridled magnitude of this woman's audacity seemed to have no parallel. By the shine of her eyes it was plain she was laughing, aware of his amazement and thoroughly enjoying it. Frank's mouth tightened up. "You can't stay here. This place belongs –"

"I don't expect he'll be usin' it."

It was that easy indifference, her total disregard for established forms and conventions, that riled Frank the most. This was a man's business here and she had no right mixing into it. Her eyes defied him to say so.

He said, trying to keep the outrage out of
104

his voice, "Squatting's one thing. Jumping preempted land –"

"You're wastin' your time."

Frank tried hard to hold onto his temper. "You don't understand –"

"Name's Larren – Sandrey," she said, her sage-colored eyes bold.

"The point –" he began.

Again she cut him off, "Seems like Brackley mentioned –"

"You know Jace?" Frank was astonished.

Her mouth widened again. Her hands strayed over her hips, bringing out more noticeably the wild grace and suppleness of that strong body. Then she was laughing up at him. "You might almost say I was Jace Brackley's widow."

Will Church left town in an ungovernable rage some half an hour ahead of Chip Gurden's return from that mysterious ride Chavez had told Frank about. Will was shaking with fury and ran his horse the entire way, even flogging the foam-flecked animal around the last hairpin twist of the trail. Coming down off the slope about twelve minutes short of dawn he saw the black oblongs of his father's headquarters buildings. The yellow squares of two lamplit windows proved Sam Church was already up. Will cursed viciously. Not one damned thing had come off as he had planned since he had tangled with Frank Carrico.

He'd got no satisfaction from Gurden. Frank had made a fool of him and those clabberheads he'd trusted with carrying out the stampede had run the goddam steers through town – or would have if Frank hadn't broken it up. True, Will's friends could still get away with some beef, but it had been Will's intention to get Kimberland blamed. If the raid had been pulled off as planned, those stampeded steers would have been spread across Bar 40 and the shortages, when discovered, would have involved W. T. in more than just suspicion.

Will rowelled the staggering horse around the house, dropping off at the back porch, leaving the spent beast standing. Sari Church was bent over the stove frying mush; Sam was just sitting down. He started to work up a growl but Will cut him off.

"Get yourself another flunky – I've took all of your crap I'm takin'." He sloshed coffee into a mug and was turning to put the pot back when his father said, glaring:

"If you've quit me again you'll walk out of here strapped."

"Strapped!" Will wheeled with such violence he lost half the cup's contents. "All

I ever *been* is strapped." Then he grinned, maliciously enjoying this. "Frank quit our ranch. He's already gone – and so are them cattle you had at Bospero Flats. They didn't stray. I found horse tracks!"

Sam Church pushed away from the table. He was reaching for his gun belt from the back of the chair when Will said, "You might as well forget them. Frank's packin' Ashenfeldt's star." He laughed at his father's expression. "Your good friend Kimberland has crossed us up."

"What's that supposed to mean?"

"Just what it sounds like. He's makin' his push."

Sam Church's cheeks looked as gray as a bullet. "Where –?"

"The best place to start," Will said, "is Terrapin. Brackley was killed in town last night."

Sam Church sagged back in his chair, mouth twitching. "The killer," Sam said, "who done it?"

Will shrugged. "Who wanted that place? If you ain't feelin' up to it, I'll ride over. Sooner we know how things stand, the better we'll know how to cope with that pirate – wouldn't surprise me at all to find he got those steers we had over at the Flats. It's his badge Frank's wearin', an' him that tolled Frank away from there."

The old man seemed lost. "We better be gettin' ourself's some gun-hands –"

"I'll take care of that," Will said.

"Where'll you get 'em?"

"There's guns around that can be picked up –"

"Drifters! Saddle tramps!"

"What the hell you expect? A Wild Bill Hickok!"

"We could do with a few like him," Church said, and Will secretly smiled. He reached over to the stove and filled his mug up again.

His mother said, "This grub's gettin' cold." Neither of them paid her the slightest attention. Will and old Sam were staring hard at each other.

Will said, "I can get us a man that's mighty near good as Hickok."

Church snorted.

"Tularosa." Will grinned.

Sam Church got halfway out of his chair. He let the shout that was in him fall back unuttered. He didn't like any better than Will did Kimberland's recent insulting demand that Will keep away from his daughter. His eyes turned craftily. In that moment he almost admired Will. "How much'll it cost an' how soon can we get him?"

Tularosa, Will was thinking, could iron out a lot of things. Including Chip Gurden, if he were offered enough. "If you'll put up a thousand dollars –"

Sam really unwound. He wasn't half through when Will headed for the door. "Where you off to?" Sam shouted. Will took hold of the latch. Sam jumped to his feet. "Now you listen to me, boy –"

"Don't *boy* me!" Will whirled in mid-stride. His eyes glared like a crazy man's. "Keep your damn money!" He slammed out of the house.

He wanted a fresh mount but rather than tote the saddle he dragged the reluctant roan he had ruined half across the hard-packed yard. Suddenly turning toward the horse with an almost incoherent fury, Will snatched up a length of chain off the ground and struck the horse over the head. The roan, screaming, reared back with bared teeth, showing the whites of his eyes. The reins were torn from Will's hand.

But the horse was too hurt to get away from him. Doubling the chain Will leaped for him, cursing. The chain struck the horse back of the withers, dropping him. Making broken, piteous, whickering sounds, the horse staggered up with a heave and stood trembling. Will lashed out again. The horse screamed like a woman. He went down in the front, and then the whole of him was down.

Will watched for a moment the feeble scrabbling of hind legs, then flung the bloody chain at him. He was hunting around for something else to lay hand to when Sam came out of the house on the run. The old man stared at the horse then at Will. He saw the shocked faces watching Will from the cook shack. He said tiredly, "What kind of man are you?" and Will's darting eyes, so frequently filled with affronted resentment, glared back with the look of a coiling snake.

"If I give you your way," Sam Church said, hating the sound of it, "what guarantee –"

Will, chopping him off, threw his shout at the men staring out of the cook shack. "Get away from that door!"

The faces faded. Will, breathing hard, walked up to his father, fists clubbed at his sides. "Take a look at yourself if you don't like what you see, an' then get out of my way. I'm through takin' your orders. This ain't the only big spread in the Panhandle. I can find other backers."

Will's head was filled with the sound of his voice. It seemed to travel all through him like the fire of raw whisky. He felt seven feet tall, rough as rock and twice as impregnable. Nothing could touch him. Nothing ever would again; and he wondered with a sense of incredulous astonishment why he had taken so long to break his father's authority.

He caught the glassy look of Sam's stare and laughed, exulting when Church cringed away from him.

Will considered the man with amused contempt. "You've tramped so long in Kimberland's shadow you act like the rest of these fetchers and carriers, but I tell you the man can be handled. Gurden's goin' after him and while they're peckin' away at each other we can take over this country!" Will make a sudden discovery. "A man gets what he's big enough to take." He liked the sound of that and said it again with a whinny of laughter.

Sam shook his head. "You're forgettin' Frank Carrico."

Anger darkened Will's skin. "He'll die just as quick of a bullet as Kimberland." Arrogance showed in the swirl of his temper. His hands, convulsing, became intolerant fists. "We'll start with these hills. We'll take the Bench right away. Go fetch me that money."

CHAPTER EIGHT

Frank at Terrapin, caught hold of her roughly. "Brackley's widow! What kind of talk's that?"

"Straight." Sandrey shook the hair back out of her face. "Why do you suppose he was in town last night?" When Frank, still scowling, said he'd gone in to see Gurden, the girl said, faintly smiling, "He came to meet me."

Frank stepped back, puzzled.

"It's true!" she said sharply. Frank's eyes called her liar. In all the years he'd known Brackley there'd been no mention of a woman. Besides this girl was too young – where could she have met up with him? "I don't know what your game is –" Frank said.

"There isn't any game. I came here in good conscience. He sent me the money. We were going to be married."

Frank looked at her sourly. "Where'd you know him before?"

"I didn't. He got my name out of a Heart-and-Hand magazine." Color whipped into

112

her lifted face. She looked at him defiantly. "People do such things –"

"Some might – if they was desperate enough."

"How do you know Jace wasn't desperate?" Her eyes were dark now and bitter, the whole look of her taut as stretched hide. "It makes no difference to me what you think. I've got his letters. I've got a deed to this place!"

Frank's eyes became unreadable.

"A quitclaim deed to it and everything on it, signed over to me in Brackley's own hand!"

"I reckon you have," Frank said finally.

She didn't seem to like the tone of his voice. "I saw Jace right after Will Church jumped him last night. He took me over to the hotel – that's when he wrote it. He got me a room; got pen and paper from the clerk – that pockmarked one with the warts on his chin. He'll remember."

Frank nodded. He could understand how Brackley might have done it, especially if the man believed that talk about Bar 40. The thing that Frank couldn't figure was this girl. On the face of it – to someone ignorant of local conditions – Brackley's ranch might hold a certain appeal. But Sandrey Larren – Frank shook his head. He had seen a couple of these Lonely Heart females, and the only resemblance between them and her wasn't showing. Why, with her shape and looks. . . .

"I've got a right to this place."

"Ma'am," he said, "I ain't disputing it. The graves are filled with folks who had rights. You'll move, one way or another."

"It's up to you to protect me."

"Then come into town where I might have some luck at it."

"I'm stayin' right here."

Suddenly fed up with this jawing, Frank said, "Why don't you try being reasonable for a change?"

She grinned. "I can take care of myself."

Frank reached out and got hold of her, roughly yanking her toward him as though by force he'd disprove her contention, revealing it beyond argument for the empty brag it was. But he had reckoned without the vulnerability of emotion. Contact roused forgotten hungers. By the time he realized what lay ahead, the lesson he'd been going to teach had gotten out of hand.

She came against him solidly. He had a wild thought of Honey, then Sandrey's breath rushed across his cheeks. Her mouth found his with astonishing firmness. The yard dissolved. Sensation blurred. It was just like crashing through the roof of the sky.

114

When they broke apart Frank was breathing hard. Everything around him tipped and spun like the way things would look from a pitching bronc. It was like coming up from the bottom of a spill.

"Well!"

The word winged toward him through incalculable space. Frank found her then, found her flushed and trembling. The breath was sawing in and out of the both of them. Sudden guilt barreled through him. His face got hot. He felt sweat come out on him. "Sandrey," he said through the roaring in his ears, "I sure didn't aim to pull anything like that!"

Her eyes were like coal in the awful whiteness of her face. He had handled her like a whore, and remembrance of Honey was like a knife twisting in him.

That was when she hit him, open-handed across the face.

He staggered back with stinging cheeks, blinking, not finding it in him to much blame her though. His blurry eyes picked her out again and he stared unbelieving. But that girl wasn't fooling. She was heading for the rifle. Frank piled onto his horse and got out of there....

He didn't know how long he rode. He felt meaner than a twitch-eyed centipede with

115

chilblains. He didn't want to think about her and wasn't hardly able to consider anything else. Except, now and then, Honey. He sure couldn't leave Sandrey Larren here in the middle of what looked to have all the makings of a knock-down and drag-out.

Frank swore. It wasn't Kimberland who Sandrey would have to fear, but the riffraff these hills were full of – the scum who might or might not be teamed up with Gurden. W. T. might grab the land but these renegades would grab Sandrey. It turned Frank sick to think what might happen if some of that crew chanced to come on her out there – rifle or no rifle!

He abruptly discovered he was no longer alone. There was a fellow up ahead on a black-and-white knothead, and the horse wasn't moving. The man wasn't, either. He was watching Frank sharply with a hand on his gun butt. He caught the flash of Frank's star and sat back, smiling sour-like, saying:

"Some pretty hard cases sifting around through these parts. Thought you might be one of them." He was garbed in an out-of-press store suit but hadn't the air or manners of a dude. He looked perfectly at home in flat-heeled boots that laced up the front, and had a turned-sideways nose below a pair of cagey eyes.

"Looking for something?" Frank asked conversationally.

"I been looking for snow but it keeps getting hotter." The fellow blew out his breath and wiped his face with a coat sleeve. "How far are we from Vega?"

"Pretty fair piece. Nearer South Fork. About a forty minute push if you happen to be in a hurry."

"It can wait," the other said. "I'm just ambling around. Expect you know most of the stockmen hereabouts?"

"Most of them." Frank could be cagey too. This guy was no tramp. Kind of hard man to place. Didn't look like a range dick. "What's your angle?"

"Just taking things easy." The fellow dug a couple of cigars from his coat, considering their tatters. Frank shook his head and the man put one back. He seemed to reach a decision. "Whereabouts does the Brackley spread lay from here?"

"Which one?" Frank said blandly.

The stranger scratched a match on the horn of his saddle. He lapped the tatters and presently, blowing smoke, broke the match stick and dropped it. "Didn't figure there was more than one."

"How long you been ramming around through these hills?"

117

The man faintly grinned. "I guess that's a fair question." He didn't seem in any great sweat to answer it.

Frank asked: "What's your business?"

The man observed brightly, "That's a marshal's badge, ain't it?"

Frank whipped his gun out. "You sooner talk here or in town?"

The man grinned. "Guess there ain't no reason you shouldn't be let in on it, everything considered. "I'm advance scout for a survey crew." Observing Frank's skepticism, he added reluctantly, "Like to keep this confidential if I can. There's some notion of putting a railroad through here."

"Keep talking."

The man shrugged. "Pretty definite now. One of your local men – fellow named Kimberland – has a wad of jack tied up in the deal. You can see why we'd want to keep it quiet for a while."

"You mean options?"

"Well – yes."

"Giving the big frogs a chance to get fixed, eh?"

The man said, "I'm not running the Company."

Frank asked, "Going to bring your road across the Bench, eh?"

"A road's got to be practicable if it aims to make money."

"Brackley's dead," Frank said. "Killed in town last night." Now Frank could understand why Brackley had been killed.

The man kept his face straight but there was a shifting back of his eyes like smoke. Frank picked up his reins.

The man rubbed his nose. "Somebody'll probably take it over."

"It won't be Gurden," Frank said pointedly.

CHAPTER NINE

Dust-splashed and taciturn Frank pulled into South Fork at a little past eleven. After studying the street he wheeled into the gloom of Fentriss' stable. The bald-headed proprietor came up, mopping at his face. Frank, getting down, allowed that he was minded to look over the spare mounts. They went out to the corrals which showed evidence of repairs. Frank considered a blue roan, a squatter, that was fifteen hands without a patch of white on her.

Fentriss leaned on his hay fork. "You fixin' to buy or borrer?"

"Rent," Frank said, and stood silent a moment. "Get her ready," he said, and abruptly walked off.

Back in the street's sun glare Frank passed up the jail, went by the hotel and, ignoring the stares of a couple of townsmen, cut over to the New York Cafe and stepped in. He took one of the twelve empty stools at the counter and distributed a part of his weight on his elbows. The pungent aroma of corned beef and cabbage made a strong bid for notice in the overheated room. At a corner table near the end of the counter Old Judge, hunched over his plate like a dilapidated vulture, sat gumming his food in preoccupied silence. "How's tricks?" Frank asked. The old man ignored him.

The biscuit-shooter, wiping hands on her apron, came from the back and hung out a tired smile. "Hi, Frank – what'll it be?"

"Slab of pie – make it apple, and a mug of black java."

The girl poured the coffee and slid the pie in front of him. He drank half the coffee at one gulp and then said, sniffing, "I'll take a bowl of that soup." The hasher dipped and passed it. "Crackers?"

Frank shook his head.

"How does it feel to be totin' the tin?"

"About like the pea in this bowl of hot water. Better give me them crackers." She pushed a plate down the counter and Frank broke up a big handful. The girl came back and leaned over, stacking some cups under the counter. She straightened up. "Thought you'd be eatin' with Honey Kimberland this noon."

Frank said, "It ain't noon yet." He finished the bowl and swung around to Old Judge. "What was you and Chip Gurden finding so profitable talking about last night?"

Old Judge, suddenly strangling, took on like a bronc with a clot of hay in its gullet. The hasher hurried over with a glass of water. "Watch out," Frank said, "you'll rust his pipes with that stuff." When the judge came up for air, Frank said, "Now that you've got that off your chest, how about answering my question?"

The old man wiped his mouth and eyes. "I don't know what you're talking about."

"It's about the size of a plaster on Terrapin. You don't have to play so innocent. That lien, if he's got one, ain't worth the paper it's written on. You can tell him I said so."

The judge, a bit shaky, got out of his chair.

He appeared so disturbed by what Frank had said to him he went off without leaving the price of his meal. Frank tossed the girl some silver and dug into his pie. She dropped it into the till and said, half indignant, "He's like to be sick for the rest of the day!"

"Do him good." Frank finished the pie, paid and grinned up at her. "Don't worry about Judge. Next to Chip Gurden he's got the strongest gut in town." He took a look at the clock. It said ten of twelve. Frank went out and settled his shoulders against the front of the place in the shade of its overhang. He saw a kid pushing a hoop coming toward him from one of the alleys. Frank dragged a sleeve over his star and tried to think about Honey, but all he could see was the face of that sorreltop he'd left out at Brackley's. Chavez came into the street on his horse from the direction of Halbertson's. They considered each other and Chavez cut over.

The Mexican said, "Pretty quiet," and then leaned out from the saddle. "Them trail hands is raisin' a hell of a stink. Claim Kimberland's back of that run-off last night; say a lot of their stuff has got mixed in with his. If that's right there's somethin' fishy, they was headed the other way. And they're still throwin' fits about all that dropped beef."

"What become of it?"

"Well," Chavez grinned, "you can't prove it by me. But a lot of people around here is goin' to really fill up today."

He rode on. The kid wabbled his hoop up to the front of the cafe, regarding Frank with bright eyes. "Got a note fer you, mister." He dug a bit of paper from his jeans and passed it over. Frank tossed back a quarter. "Geez!" the kid yelled, and tore off like a twister.

Frank looked at the note. Signed "Kelly," it read: *Be in front of the bakeshop today at 12 noon.*

Frank peered through the window. Two minutes. He recalled the message Gurden's piano thumper had left for him with Danny, about some deal Kelly was in with Chip. Wants to explain that, he thought, and shook his head. Nothing, anymore, was solid white or solid black. Everybody it seemed was daubed with something. Everyone but Honey. In another half hour they'd be putting on the nosebag.

He struck off toward the bake shop. He wasn't going to have much time with Honey for at one o'clock he was due to take over patrolling the town; and he still hadn't figured what to do about Sandrey. He wistfully remembered the job he had quit and halfway wished himself back at Bospero

Flats where life, though dull, had been simply a routine matter of eating, sleeping and watching cows' butts while they fed on the landscape. He had frequently bemoaned in those halcyon days being maneuvered into the position of being Will Church's keeper – now he was saddled with an entire town. Frank was out of his depth and he finally knew it.

He was abreast of Abbie Burks' millinery, with the bake shop's front in plain sight when, just like a hand had reached out to stop him, something pulled Frank up. He looked around perplexedly, and so discovered Kimberland riding in from the south. The Bar 40 boss waved, calling out some rigamarole which Frank, at this distance, couldn't make head nor tail of.

Frank got to within thirty feet of the rancher when Krantz, vastly excited, bulged around the near end of his store. "Gott in Himmel!" he gasped, floundering up to Frank and catching hold of him. His eyes were like peeled grapes behind the lenses of his spectacles. "Kvick – com kvick," he urged, wheezing. "In the back of mine blace you should see –"

W. T. Kimberland's shadow fell across the storekeeper. It seemed like Krantz's breath slid even farther out of reach. Sweat gleamed on his cheeks like lard.

"What's up?" Kimberland said, eyeing him curiously.

Krantz glared. "It shouldn't happen to a dog!" He tugged at Frank's arm and Frank let the man pull him back into the alley.

Kimberland swung down, moving after them. "Someone get hurt?"

The remark angered Frank. Krantz hauled him around the back end of the Mercantile toward a welter of boxes out of which barrel staves thrust like a scatter of rib bones.

The marshal's eyes widened. It was Gurden's piano man. With his neck folded over a crate top and his button-shoed legs flopped out of its bottom he lay like a drunk in the last stages of stupor. His brown derby, upended, lay a few feet beyond him with a break in its crown. Frank saw his head then. One look was enough.

"God above!" Kimberland muttered. "What'd they do – beat his brains out?" He backed off looking bilious, half lifting an arm as though to defend himself. "Who'd do a thing like that – and for what?"

Frank eyed the storekeeper. "You got any ideas?"

Krantz, making retching sounds, turned away and was sick. Frank ran back to the street, his eyes searching for Chavez while he thought of Sandrey alone out at Brackley's.

Kimberland caught up with him. "This is a terrible thing –"

Frank turned on him, snarling. "What are you fixing to do to this country?"

The Bar 40 man was taken aback. Now a dark core of watchfulness got into his stare. "Why, Frank, all I've ever done is try to improve this miserable country."

"You think that railroad's going to be any good to it?"

The man stared thoughtfully. "So you know about that." A little silence piled up, and then he said, speaking earnestly, "Of course it will. It's bound to! We'll be a shipping point instead of just another two-bit town upon the trail. Hell, I've put my money into it – every cent I could spare. I've even borrowed to bring that road here!" He swung his arms. "There'll be a great future –"

"You mean for them Benchers, or just for yourself?"

Kimberland let his arms drop. He stepped back, looking startled. But he covered it, chuckling. "Thought for a moment you meant that."

Frank caught sight of Chavez then and

waved him toward the back of Krantz's place. Chavez nodded. Frank looked at Kimberland. "How are you figuring to benefit them Benchers?"

"Frank, talk sense," Kimberland said.

Frank sent his glance over the street, out into the hot glare, observing the sand-scoured fronts of the buildings, oddly surprised to find no change in their appearance. Birds were still chirping. Only in himself was the film of winter's ice apparent, crackling out its warning, skewering him with a million needles. His eyes, hard as jade, found Kimberland's face. "My Dad was one of those Benchers."

Kimberland was silent, a shade tighter of lip but obviously considering, casting up his impressions with that same cold assurance which had carried him through every bind in his life. He said, very softly, "Don't get in my way, Frank."

It was the man's attitude, as much as it was anything, which brought all of Frank's anger into sudden sharp focus.

Kimberland growled, "Don't be a damned fool!"

A mounting crest of excitement was in Frank now, the walls of his confusions crumbling away. The sheen of Kimberland's eyes, the pinched-in look about his mouth, was ample warning. But he said, thinly smiling, "I'm not fool enough to think I'll ever be able to pin anything on you," and saw the answering glint, the triumph and satisfaction which looked out of the cattleman's eyes. "But," said Frank, tapping a finger against W. T.'s chest, "if you molest those Benchers in any way I'm coming after you, mister."

CHAPTER TEN

It was good while he'd been at it but, watching the Bar 40 boss ride off toward the hotel, Frank understood the futility of using such talk on a man like Kimberland. A kind of baying at the moon. W. T. Kimberland was king in his country.

All the confidence and good feeling was washed out of Frank, leaving nothing behind but cold emptiness. The whole shadowy pack of old worries closed round him. He forgot his surroundings in this grim absorption. Kimberland's influence would rip the star off him –

He felt the breath of the bullet before the report of the shot slapped the fronts of the buildings. Frank dropped, yanking his sixshooter, rolling frantically for the alley mouth. A slug kicked splinters off the corner above his head. He was beginning to believe he was going to reach shelter when something with the shock of a forty-pound sledge slammed him into the wall.

He shot twice from that position at the disappearing back of a man fading around the far side of Fentriss' stable. Frank got his legs under him and lurched to his feet. The whole left side of his chest felt numb. There were calls and questions as men piled out of the nearest doorways, but Frank hardly noticed. He ran across the street, cutting east of the stable since the man obviously would not be crazy enough to try to escape through that open stretch west of it.

At the back of the place he looked in both directions and saw no sign of the man. It did not seem reasonable to assume he'd reached cover in so short a time without somebody seeing him. The fellow's very haste would have attracted attention. So he must be in the stable. Shutting his eyes for a moment Frank dived through the side door. His gun was ready but there was nothing to fire at; he could see well enough to have spotted movement. He yelled for Fentriss.

The man came in from the pens. "I've

got her ready – What happened to your badge?"

Frank looked down at it blankly. "Where is he? Where'd he go to?"

"If I knowed what you was talkin' about –"

"Tularosa! Didn't you see him?"

"No – and I don't want to!" Fentriss growled.

"He must be hiding around here some-place."

"Then I'll be back when he's left."

Frank said, swearing, "You can help me look, can't you?"

"No, sir! I ain't about to look for no killer!" He grabbed both hands to his hat and backed out of the place.

Frank got to work. He went over that stable with a fine-toothed comb, he checked the pens outside, but he did not find Tularosa. He was minded to swear in a posse but knew as well as he knew his own name how much good he could expect from that. They would all be like Fentriss. It was Frank they'd pinned the star on. It was up to Frank to catch Tularosa.

Still fisting the gun he moved out back of the jail, alert and still edgy, but taking enough time to examine the ground. There were plenty of tracks, most of them too recent to pick out the ones he was hunting. Tularosa must have been past here. Next door was the hotel and beyond that Halbertson's hay shed. Then the shacks where the bulk of this town had their homes. He wouldn't have a Chinaman's chance singlehanded. Someone was almost bound to have seen the man but Frank could understand no one was going to admit it.

Chavez caught sight of Frank and cut over. "I heard the shots," he said, "but I was prowling the lumber yard. What happened to your badge?"

Frank eyed the bent metal. "Another half inch and that slug would of got me." He looked frowningly back in the direction of those shacks. Chavez, reading his mind, said, "I'm game if you want to try it, but the chances are he's pulled his freight."

"I suppose," Frank scowled, and then caught sight of his shadow. "Hell!" He suddenly remembered Honey Kimberland. "I'll take over at one."

He hurried back to the stable and, twisting the stirrup, stepped into the saddle. "Takin' off?" Fentriss said, and Frank looked down at him. "I'll be around. Seen any more of that herd boss?"

"Man, is he hot!" Fentriss passed up the blue roan's reins. "They're out combin' the

131

breaks. Sent one of his hands after Draicup. If that jasper comes back with them wild men of his we're like to –"

But Frank, just now, wasn't interested in Draicup. He stopped by the jail but didn't see the jailer. Already late, he was about to move on when Chavez swung into sight between buildings, shotgun cradled across his knees. Frank cut over, repeating the gist of his powwow with Kimberland. "If you want out, say so."

"Ha!" Chavez grinned. "Have you found a good hole to crawl into?"

Frank scowled. "Where's Danny?"

"Ain't seen him. If he ain't over to the jail he's probably feedin' his face."

Frank said, "If anything comes up you'll find me doing the same, at the hotel." He sent the roan toward its rack. He got down and walked into the lobby. Bernie, the gun-shop man, put down his wrinkled copy of the Dallas paper and tossed Frank a nod. "Anything new?" Frank grunted, not seeing Honey, and went along to the cigar case where he treated himself to the luxury of a ten-center. He bit the end from the weed and put his back against the show-case. "Soon as I get through here I'm going after Chip Gurden."

Bernie looked at him sharply. He was a

heavy-set man with a well-fed look, one of the town's more substantial citizens with a home in Snob Hollow and a bank account that, by some people's tell of it, would have choked a grown herd sire. Bernie studied Frank's countenance. "Think Draicup will be back?"

In the way he put the question there was an undertow of worry that brought Tularosa back into Frank's thinking. "I don't know," Frank said, frowing. "I can't see why he would though. Gourd and Vine troubles ain't no skin off his nose."

"Maybe," Bernie said, "you better get W. T. to let you deputize some of his crew. Just in case," he added grimly.

Neither man noticed the tap of heels on the stairs, neither of them saw the arrested shape of the girl. She was off to one side above the level of Bernie's chair and Frank was too much worked up to take his glance away from the saddle merchant. He said uncomfortably but with an edge of defiance, "I don't think Kimberland's in any mood to oblige me."

Bernie's glance was puzzled. "Put you in, didn't he?"

Frank had always known this town kowtowed to Kimberland just as the smaller stockmen did. When there weren't any trail

133

herds, Bar 40 and its satellites – Arnold and the Churches – were the standby of these shop keepers, all that kept them going. Frank wondered if they guessed what Kimberland was up to. Probably not. Like enough they wouldn't give a damn. But he had to try. He said, "There's been a –"

"Been a what?"

Frank wondered how he could make Bernie see this when it wasn't even clear in his own mind. "Those fellers on the Bench –"

"Trash!" the merchant said contemptuously. "They wouldn't know a fine gun if it hit 'em in the eye!"

The clerk, back of Frank, put his oar in. "Except for Brackley puttin' that woman up here last night we've never got a nickel's worth of business off the bunch of them – and don't look to, I can tell you."

"Well, a man has to make a living," Frank said. "But –"

"Look," Bernie scowled. "There's good grass on that Bench. This drop in the market's caught Bar 40 over-stocked. There ain't a man in this town would honestly blame W. T. if he took over that whole range. It's too bad about Brackley but you can't –"

"I did," Frank said, and squared his shoulders. "It's not a question of grass.

134

Kimberland wants that whole Bench and I've warned him to stay away –"

"Why, you damned fool!" Bernie leaped from his chair, white and shaking with outrage. "Kimberland's practically *made* this town! If it wasn't for him –"

Frank suddenly discovered Honey on the stairs. The expression on his face and the direction he was staring pulled the saddle man's head around.

Red faced, still glowering, Bernie dragged off his hat. "Your servant, ma'am, and pardon...." He let the rest trail off with another black glare at the marshal.

Never had the girl looked more desirable to Frank. Looking down at them she held her head a little back, some trick of light on that shadowed stair bringing out the delicate structure of her face, heightening its proud beauty beneath the gleam of spun-gold hair so that she seemed the very embodiment of all that was fine and farthest from Frank's reach.

He wasn't bucking her old man so much because of what Kimberland was cooking up as because of the way the man hoped to come at it, treating those Benchers like a pack of damn Indians. Not that Frank liked them or they liked him. They were a stiffnecked bunch of penniless polecats, too cross-

grained to work and too shiftless to neighbor
with, but Frank wasn't going to see them
shoved off their places just because they were
trash in the eyes of these moguls. He had
been trash himself until this star pulled him
out of it. In their books, anyway.

A brightness came into his look, peering
up at her. There was no hesitation in the way
she faced Bernie. A kind of smile had parted
her lips, deepening their color against her
pale cheeks. Not many could have carried off
so well the unenviable position in which
Frank's words had placed her. His thoughts
embraced this with relief and in humility as
he sensed the gathering fierceness with
which she meant to defend him. He could
now admit, within the privacy of his
perceptions, that he had been a little worried.
Yet he had known she would understand; she
could not have been herself, the guiding light
of all Frank's reaching – the very core of
every dream – and acted differently. To have
shown less compassion than himself was
plain unthinkable.

Frank's heart swelled with pride. It gave
him the courage to say, "They've got some
rights, too. They're not animals, Bernie."

The merchant half lifted a shaking fist, so
furious it seemed as though he must burst.
He twisted his glowering red face up at

Honey. "You going to listen to that kind of guff? Bring this fool to his senses or –"

Honey giggled. Her eyes encountered Frank's and she laughed right out, uncontrollably. "Oh dear –" she gasped, blinking, holding onto her side. "Of course he's a fool. A bumptious, ignorant, spur-clacking nobody! Why else do you suppose Father gave him that star!"

CHAPTER ELEVEN

Frank stood like a man in the clutch of paralysis. Each contraction of his heart held the impact of a fist. He had a giddy sense of motion, of being alone on some high point with the wind rushing round him and nothing to catch hold of.

He drew a ragged breath and his stare found Bernie. The man's face hung in mottled folds against the bones which upheld it. His eyes bulged like the eyes of a frog. Now his lips writhed away from the rotten stumps of teeth locked together.

It was the clerk's hysterical grip on Frank's shoulder which finally got through to him, bringing him out of it. He let go of

Bernie's throat, saw the clerk's scared face and shoved the man stumbling out of his path. He went through the door blindly and onto the porch. All he could see was Honey's face tight with scorn. Breath began to come into him. He saw this town as the place really was. The fault was his for imagining he could pull himself up by his bootstraps.

He jammed fists in pockets and felt the crackle of paper. *Kelly's note.* He glanced at his shadow, checked the guess by his watch. Too late. His eyes raked the dusty glare of the street, noting its emptiness while a resolve solidified behind the tough planes of his cheeks.

Chavez came along heading west toward the office. "I'll take over," Frank said.

Chavez nodded. "Somethin' I don't savvy back there." He flung a dissatisfied look over his shoulder. "Could of swore I heard a woman yell."

Chavez was a bundle of contradictions. His mother, dead in childbirth, had been with a road show which had gone to pieces in Dalhart. She had put herself beyond forgiveness by marrying his father, a Mexican horse breaker who'd been working for Sam Church at the time. Frank had heard several versions of the story but all agreed Church had hounded the man out of the

138

country. Frank could imagine what Chavez's boyhood had been with a father tossed from pillar to post and the blood of two races forever clashing inside him.

"Where was this?" Frank asked, scowling.

"Passing the bake shop. Could of been wrong. Might of been that hasher at the New York Cafe. Could of been a horse."

"My worry," Frank said, and crossed over to Gurden's. The gambler, back of the bar, had both arms anchored to a spread-open newspaper. He looked up, face tightening, as Frank stepped in. At this slack time, in addition to Gurden and one of his dealers laying out a hand of sol, there were only three other men, local customers, in the place. Frank didn't miss the way these quit talking.

"Where's Mousetrap, Gurden?"

The saloon owner shrugged. "When he ain't on duty his time's his own." He plopped the butt of his stogie into a spittoon. "Shall I say you been lookin' for him?"

"I've got a cell looking for him if I happen to lay hands on him, and I wouldn't be surprised but what I can find room for you. Why are these gents toting guns in your place?"

"Now look –"

"You know the law. You helped make it."

Frank continued to stare until the

saloonman's face showed his hate and fury. When the stillness threatened to become too oppressive Frank waved a hand at the three bellying the bar. "Uncinch that hardware."

There were black looks and grumbling but the men complied.

"Now pick up your belts and head for the jail."

"You ain't serious –"

"By the time you get out you'll be a better judge of that." Frank waited till the men reluctantly started for the batwings, then he said, "You're through in South Fork, Gurden. You cut your string too short with Willie. The next stage leaves at seven o'clock. Be on it, and take your hired thugs with you."

After he'd locked the men up, Frank, recalling what Chavez had told him, got his mare from the hotel hitchrack, got aboard and pointed her east. At the stage depot he crossed the road's sun-scorched dust and stepped down in front of the New York Cafe. The place had no business.

The hasher was fanning herself back of the counter. She gave him a withering look. "You've shot your bolt, takin' up for them Benchers. I guess this heat must've scrambled your brains."

140

Frank managed a grin. "You can't scramble something you don't have to start with. Let's have another cup of that varnish you call java."

"And then tellin' Gurden to get out of town! You got a hankerin' for a coffin?"

"How the hell did you hear about that?"

"I heard it," she said. "The whole town's buzzin'."

Frank sagged onto a stool and tiredly leaned on his elbows. "Chip was after me anyhow."

She poured the coffee and put it in front of him. "Bernie ain't about to make no sheep's eyes at you – what'd you want to rough him up for? And Kimberland, too." She put her hands on her hips. "What you need is darn good talkin' to."

Frank saucered some of his coffee and held it up to blow at. "Seen Kelly around?"

"Kelly! Man, you better get your sights set on steerin' clear of Gurden."

"You been here all morning, ain't you?"

She shook her head like she was giving Frank up. "You know darn well I have. You think that Greek would let me outa this joint?"

"You hear anything a while ago? Like maybe some woman was yelling or something?"

141

She wiped her cheeks with her apron and regarded him queerly.

"Reason I asked, Chavez thought he heard something last time he was by here. You know if Abbie Burks is home?"

She started to sniff then shook her head, looking paler. She leaned forward abruptly. "Danny Settles was over behind her place a while ago. . . . I know because I saw him. Jake'll tell you the same. He seen him, too."

Frank got down off the stool and stepped into the kitchen.

"That's right," the Greek said. He pushed a pan of dough back and wiped floured hands on his shirt front. "Skulkin', he was. I said so then and I'll say so now. Squintin' back over his shoulder an' all scrounch down like he was scairt someone would see him. Hell of a guy you should pick for a jailer. Right back of that brush," he pointed, "that's where I seen him."

Frank stepped out the back door. He went over to the brush and started looking around. In an alkaline spot that wasn't haired over with grass he saw fresh sign, the print of a boot heel. He found where this party had worked through the brush on a line with Abbie's back door.

He went over there and knocked without getting any answer. He tried the latch but the

142

door was barred. "Abbie?" He jiggled the thing but no one moved inside the house.

"An' I'll tell you somethin' else," the Greek said grimly when Frank returned. "It won't be the first time that feller's been over there."

Frank went out to the mare and then went back to ask, looking troubled, "How long ago was this?"

"Well –" the hasher said, "it's been a couple of hours, I guess. About the time of that shootin', give or take a few minutes."

Of course, Frank thought. Knowing Abbie, he knew she'd take Danny in when he was probably scared half out of what wits he had left by those shots Frank had swapped with that damned Tularosa. Danny had gone to Abbie with the trust of a frightened dog. But why had she yelled – or had she? "You reckon she's out?"

The hasher couldn't give him any help there. "I never *seen* her go, if that's what you mean."

Frank went back to the street. He didn't want to break in. He'd look a pretty fool if Abbie was home.

He walked over to the mare. Abbie might have plenty of reasons for not coming to the door. She might have been working. He hadn't tried the front. He was starting to walk over there when he saw John Arnold turning in at the path. Arnold, glumly preoccupied with things in his mind, went through the picket fence without noticing Frank.

It came over Frank rather oddly that Arnold's look was generally perturbed whenever he seemed to be heading for Abbie's. Perhaps the rancher only visited his niece when the cares of this world got to weighing too heavy. It was a weird thing to think and yet in no way more strange than well-off John Arnold with a prosperous ranch permitting his kin – his only kin, far as Frank knew – to spend her time making bonnets for other people's women.

He had never happened to catch this angle on it before, and now was baffled to realize that never had he heard of Abbie visiting the ranch. Frank recalled the hasher's sniff and the unexplained color with which Abbie had told him this morning that she supposed her uncle was still around. It then occurred to Frank the strain he'd always sensed in her might spring from something other than a New England parentage.

A little startled, Frank suddenly saw Abbie Burks as the women of this town had, those good housewives and mothers he'd thought resented her good looks and the fact that she was in business.

The discontinuance of Arnold's knocking fetched Frank out of this thinking and he heaved into the saddle as Arnold's steps approached around the side of the house, and suddenly stopped. Frank might have gone to see what Arnold was swearing about except that, just then, he caught sight of Kelly beckoning from the doorway of the stage barn.

Frank put the mare across the street. Kelly abruptly faded away from the door. At that moment, Frank saw the surveyor's scout he had met in the hills coming in from the west. The scout was half falling out of his saddle. Sandrey Larren, riding alongside, was doing her best to hold him on.

Forgetting Kelly, Frank swung toward them, touching the mare with the points of his spurs. A moment before, the town had seemed asleep on its feet; now men appeared from a dozen doorways – even Old Judge with a beer in his hand running out of the Flag to find out what was happening.

Frank reached the surveyor's scout and eased him down. Blood and dust were all over the front of him and his face looked like a mask of waxed paper. Sandrey's cheeks were drawn. Both horses showed lather.

Ignoring the excited jabber around him, Frank hoisted the scout and carried him into the Blue Flag where he eased him onto a faro table. It was to be seen at a glance he was no case for a sawbones; the man had lost too much blood, and there was froth on his mouth.

"Back up!" Frank growled as men crowded around them. His glance flashed to Sandrey.

She said, "Will he make it?"

Frank, studying the man, shook his head. "What happened?"

Sandrey drew a long breath. "He stopped by my place – it was just before noon. He gave this pitch about a railroad, said he wanted an easement. He came right out and offered cash money for it. I put him off, told him I'd have to talk first with my neighbors. He upped his price five hundred dollars –"

"Get to the shooting." Frank ignored the rest of them. He could tell by their looks of startled excitement this was the first they'd heard about any railroad.

Sandrey's eyes were smoky sage and she was still breathing hard. Frank understood this was emotion. She was fiercely angry. It was in all her looks, in the hand she put up to push back her hair. Her cheeks were pale but fright had nothing to do with this.

"It was the cattle," she said, "we didn't see the men right off, only the cows. They were everywhere, like a sea of horns, bawling and staring wherever we turned. They must have shoved that whole six thousand –"

"Kimberland's got more than that," Frank said.

She looked at him straightly. "You don't get it. I'm talking about – Church. Will Church."

"You must be mistaken. The cows you saw were Bar Forty –"

"Tell him!" Sandrey said; and Frank followed her glance to the pain-racked eyes staring up at him.

"That's right," the scout whispered. "Circle C the brand was."

An angry muttering broke out back of Frank. Heels fell loud across the planks of the porch, and Sandrey said, "Young Church himself – the one who threatened you last night and then lifted his hat to me – came loping up with a couple of hardcases. He was feeling pretty pleased with himself. 'Sorry,' he said, 'but you can't stay here.' Then Mr. Fles –" her hand moved toward the scout on the faro table – "told Will Church he was barking up the wrong tree, that I was owner of Terrapin. He –" she looked at Frank fiercely – "never had a chance to say anything more. Church grabbed up a pistol and shot him. It all happened so quick I couldn't keep up with it. Both of Church's men had their guns out by this time. Church said *'Git!'* and we done it. I'm pretty sure if we hadn't he'd have shot me too."

Frank could hardly believe Church had been such a fool. Yet, it was exactly what Will would do, given nerve enough. Somewhere he had found the nerve. Frank saw but two possible answers to this. Either Will had got backing for this defiance of Kimberland or, stung frantic by the loss of face he had suffered at Frank's hands, the man had gone hog wild.

There was a commotion back up front by the doors and Chavez, thin-lipped, intolerant of delay, came through the crowd blackly shoving men off his elbows. "That Burks woman has been raped and they're hangin' Danny Settles!"

CHAPTER TWELVE

They're at the stage company's barn!"
Chavez piled in the saddle. "I tried to talk
some sense into them. Arnold tried, too. You
know what a mob is! They're fixin' to use
that hay hoist...."

Frank's thoughts, and the wind, isolated
him from the rest of what the deputy was
saying. Frank was raking the mare with the
gut hooks. Every fiber of his being rebelled
against this and he cursed the loose jaws
which had incited it. Settles had been no
more capable of attacking Abbie Burks than
a cow was of singing, yet these fools in their
need to fight back at their fears...

Snarling, Frank crouched lower with the
wind in his ears as they flashed past the
storefronts, making the run in twenty-seven
seconds. He cursed the white faces that
twisted around at him. He slammed the roan
into them, scattering them. He had a blade
in his hand. He knew before she had slid to
a stop – by the grotesque way Danny spilled
to the ground – he had got here too late.

Frank appeared about ready to start killing

the handiest. The stock knife in his fist gleamed sharp as a saber and the mob fell away, shamefaced, some yelling, stumbling over each other in their fright and their guilt.

Frank dropped off the mare, bent over Danny, unashamed of the glistening blur in his lashes. It wasn't that the man had ever been close – no two could have been farther apart than the gentle dead and this roughneck marshal. Frank's emotions were aroused by the utter uselessness of this, the sheer stupidity that would allow men to act so.

Throwing off the rope he got up, bone weary, and saw Arnold's grim-set mask of a face. Behind him was Chavez with his sawed-off. The rest were gone.

"Crept away like whipped curs!" the Mexican said.

"Go tell Ben Holliday," Frank said, "we've got some more business for him." When the deputy left, Arnold said, "Man can't reason with fools." He glared at Danny and swore. "That girl was my life. Should have married her long ago. Was too damned smug," he said, hating himself, "too stinking proud of being Kimberland's right hand to chance offending. Kimberland would never have understood my marrying a kept woman."

150

Frank pulled off his neckscarf and covered Danny's face. "I blame myself."

"No need to. Danny never –"

"I know that. But I went over there and knocked. I should have broken in."

"Wouldn't have made any difference. She'd been dead for sometime. Beaten, raped – strangled. Never locked her doors. Danny said the place was locked front and back when he slipped over there. He was frightened, went for comfort. They found him in that brush back of Wolverton's after that Greek and his hasher. . . . *God!*"

A putty-faced hostler came out of the barn. "I'll watch him," he muttered.

Frank set off up the street, the mare's reins in his hand, Arnold silent beside him. There were plenty of men standing around on the walks, but no one intercepted them, no one met Frank's stare.

Arnold growled, "There's just one son of a bitch in this country – that could have done this."

"Tularosa," Frank said. "He's here, but how to find him."

"I'll find him!"

Frank told him then about the scout, and Sandrey's story.

"I've sometimes wondered," Arnold said, "if perhaps Will wasn't back of this cow-

151

stealing. Whenever the herds come through he's got money. He damn sure never got any from his father."

"I'm afraid Sam's in this. Will would never buck W. T. without help."

"He could be getting it from Gurden. That kid plays more than's good for him. Chip's got a bundle of his paper."

"I've told Gurden to pull his freight when that stage leaves tonight."

"He won't do it."

"I'm not expecting him to."

Arnold grinned at Frank bleakly. "What about W. T.?"

Frank sighed. "I reckon he'll fight."

Arnold said, "Here's where I leave you."

Kelly, when he had waved at Frank, had been minded to throw himself on Frank's mercy. He had beckoned Frank over to spill what he knew; but when Frank, distracted, had whirled his mare up the street, the teamster was left like a drowning man who has grasped at a straw and finds himself sinking.

He stared after Frank in a sweat of self-pity. Saw the reeling scout and the girl hanging onto him, but all he could think of was the look of Chip Gurden.

Desperate, outraged, half out of his head

152

with the bitter emotions of a man whose best has never been good enough, he looked again at Frank and ran back for his rifle. All the twisted hate of the man's warped nature was prodding him now with galling remembrance of how Frank had always been one step ahead of him. He picked up the rifle and returned to the entrance in time to see Frank, carrying the stranger, step through the Flag's batwings.

Kelly cursed in a frenzy, then cunning came into the wild blaze of his stare. Frank would have to come out. Be a pretty far shot. Making sure the hostler was still at his feeding, Kelly returned to the door and, cradling his Winchester, settled down where he'd be ready. There'd be no slip this time.

A growing clamor across the way gradually crept through the shell of Kelly's pre-occupation. Finally, irritably, he twisted his face around. A crowd was forming between the Bon Ton and the bake shop. Even as he watched, it broke apart and ran off in segments; but almost at once it began to regroup itself as two men came shoving another cowed shape; the sound of their voices brought Kelly out of his crouch.

They seemed to be having quite a wrangle. He saw the hasher from the New York Cafe swinging her arms about and the Greek from the same place nodding emphatically. Growing yells went up as Danny Settles was shoved to the front again and out of this uproar came the shouted word – *rope*. Kelly saw Arnold's furious features and saw Chavez break away from the crowd. Arnold dropped out of sight amid a flurry of blows and then the whole push was crossing the street. Kelly's horrified stare saw them heading straight for him. His shaking hands dropped the rifle. He ducked through the side door and clambered into his saddle, cuffing the horse with the rein ends, beating its ribs with his heels.

After Arnold left to go off somewhere on his own hook, Frank strode on to the Flag, tied his mare and went in. A few men at the bar were arguing about Danny's lynching. Frank looked at them bleakly and two or three remembered forgotten chores which took them away. Talk petered out and then Wolverton asked Frank, "What are you going to do about Church?"

"I'll take care of him." Frank bought himself a beer and watched a dealer setting up a faro layout on the scrubbed-clean table where the dead scout had lain.

McFell, the Flag's owner, wearing a brown derby and impeccably dressed as usual except for the folded newspaper protruding from his coat's left pocket, drifted in from the back and gave Frank the eye from a corner of the bar. Frank finished his beer and went over. "The young woman," McFell said, "asked me to tell you she would be at the hotel."

Frank nodded his thanks. He was in a black mood and painfully preoccupied with thoughts of his own, yet something about the other made him scrutinize McFell more closely.

McFell's lips quirked a little. "Tularosa, wasn't it?"

Frank considered this, frowning, and glanced up at the clock, astonished to find that it was near five.

McFell said, "If you was Will Church and figured to go whole hog, what would you do to copper the bet?"

Frank said quietly, "Hire that damned killer."

"I've a pretty fair hunch that's the way he's figuring."

"And how would Will get hold of him?"

McFell tipped his head to stare down at his hands. Frank guessed he was making his mind up how far he wanted to go. Still without looking up, McFell said, "I guess you know Chip's been holding a bunch of Will's IOUs. Tularosa was in Chip's back room last night before you put him in the cooler. If you was Will, and made a deal with Tularosa, what are the first two jobs you would give him?"

Frank said, "Fixing Gurden. Taking care of me."

"So," McFell said, "if you watch Chip..." and thinly smiled.

Frank went back to the street. A pair of cowhands were jogging away from Minnie's; by her door another was just quitting the saddle. Another gent was mounting in front of Fentriss' barn. Small gatherings of talkers studded the walks farther down and, closer at hand, two men alongside the damaged corner of Bernie's gun shop were eyeing him with what looked to be a somewhat strained attention.

Frank untied the roan mare and, swinging up, turned her toward them. The pair lurched apart. One of them, disappearing into the alley, was Gurden's new muscle man, Mousetrap. Frank let him go.

The other was Sam Church. He thrust out his jaw as Frank came up to him, scowling in that dog-with-a-bone way the marshal remembered. Naked malice and a number of things less easily deciphered were in his stare. "Don't come whinin' around for your money," Sam Church growled, "after the

156

way you took off from Bospero Flats – lost me ever' damn one of them beeves!"

Frank said, "Shut your old face. And you'd better snap the leash back on Will. Shooting that feller –"

Church said with a sneer, "If you had any proof –"

"I got all I need."

Malice got into the old man's choking voice, that raw edge of arrogance that was Will's stock in trade, more insufferable in Will's father, more infuriatingly caustic and contemptuous. "If you want to get laughed out of this town, go ahead. Fetch him in, if you're able. Five separate people saw that skunk reach first."

"Just who," Frank said, "are you talking about?"

"That sneak Kimberland brought in here, that feller we run into at Brackley's. Tried to gun Will down – even got off first shot." He grinned like a toothless old wolf, throwing his head back. "If you're countin' on that skirt sayin' otherwise you're a bigger damn fool than W. T. took you for. A saloon slut! Who'd believe her?" The chin jutted forward from his turkeycock neck, his red jowls jiggling like wattles. "Sake of ol' times I'm goin' to give you a tip – git out of this country while you're still able!"

Frank watched the old vinegarroon stamp into the Opal. All these years that Frank had known him the man's cupidity and miser's caution had kept him in Kimberland's string of supporters, dancing attendance on the big pot's bubbling, glad of the crumbs from the mogul's table. Something big, something thunderous, must have happened to make Sam Church think he could safely fly in the face of Kimberland's wrath to make a grab of his own at this strip W. T. coveted.

Frank followed Church as far as the Opal's porch. Now he found himself staring at one of the handbills he'd had Chavez put up to acquaint all and sundry with the new restrictions and penalties having to do with the carrying of firearms. It was crude. Butcher paper. Hand lettered with pencil.

Frank suddenly woke up. He cuffed his hat a bit lower to give more reach to his eyes. The whole look of him sharpened. A grin cracked his lips that was like summer lightning.

CHAPTER THIRTEEN

He felt the kind of weird bounce a man gets in poker when he fills to an inside straight. He'd got into this jackpot trying to impress people with abilities he didn't have. The one thing he *did* have was the rep he'd been trying to get shed of. Turbulence and violence had put the meat on his bones and it was, by damn, high time he quit selling himself short. This wasn't as rough as it looked – couldn't be! The trick was to pick away at the deal. Packing the star made a man feel naked but the forces against him were flesh and blood too, heir to the same drawbacks Frank fought. Bring it down to individuals, man to man, and the deal looked different.

He stepped onto the planks of the Opal's porch, graveled to think he hadn't seen this before.

A hail caught him back as he would have pushed into Gurden's. His glance, coming around, found Krantz and Joe Wolverton hurrying into the street from the far side of the Mercantile. Krantz, waggling an arm, broke into a run. Frank paused, undecided, then stepped through the batwings with a gun in his fist.

The place turned as quiet as the day after the Fourth. A chair scraped someplace and the stillness built around this, chunk on chunk till it was like a solid wall. Frank's stare picked up four men at the bar, a townsman at the end of it and three strangers part way down. He discovered Bill Grace at a card table with two Bar 40 punchers and the bronc stomper from X3. It was the horse-breaker's chair which had been shoved back.

Frank said, "Where's Church?"

Nobody answered but the townsman standing solo at the end of the mahogany shot a nervous glance toward the door of Chip's office. Frank's eyes raked the rest of them. "Clear out," he said, "this place has been closed."

He gave them ten seconds and when nobody moved drove a slug at the horse-breaker's chair. This collapsed with a shattered leg, spilling the X3 man to the floor. The Bar 40 punchers lurched to their feet. Bill Grace, Kimberland's foreman, got up too but he took more time to it, eyeing Frank narrowly. The horse-breaker got up looking mean-mouthed and violent. More ringy than Grace, or perhaps less observing, he permitted his resentment to prod him into speech:

"Who the hell do you think you're hoorawin'!" He started for Frank like the wrath of God. A horse-length away the fellow's feet slowed and stopped. He seemed a bit less ruddy about the gills and began to sweat.

One of the strangers at the bar curled his lip and said, "Chicken."

Frank placed these three then, guessing them to have some connection with Will Church. They were hard-bitten customers, belted and spurred, obviously looking for trouble. All three were armed.

Frank's mouth turned thin. He took a long step forward, swapping his six-shooter from right hand to left. His right closed in the front of the nearest man's shirt and fetched him around in a staggering circle, suddenly letting go of him. Momentum did the rest. The fellow crashed into his cronies, knocking one of them sideways. The other, ducking, slapped leather, but before he could bring the gun into line Frank cracked him hard across the face with his pistol.

The man fell back, yelling. He managed to jerk off one shot that brought dust off the ceiling then Frank banged his weapon across the man's wrist. The gun dropped. Frank booted it. The man reeled against the bar, sickly moaning.

The horse-breaker backed away with both hands up. The man Frank had used to break up the play lay where he had dropped, eyes bulging. There was blood across his chin. Frank said to Bill Grace, "Take all three of them over to the jail and lock 'em up. Rest of you get out of here."

He saw Gurden staring from the doorway of his office. When the last customer got off the porch, Frank stepped up to Gurden. "Got this place sold yet?"

The saloonman stood with his mouth so tight the stogie began to sag as though his teeth had gone clean through it.

"Don't wait too long. That stage leaves at seven." Frank's shoulder cut against Gurden and the flat of Frank's hand – the one that was empty – pushed Gurden's chest, and this way the saloonman was backed into his office. Frank's grin licked at Church. "You're in bad company, old man. Get Will's IOUs back yet?"

Sam Church looked about to throw a fit. Fury crept into Gurden's stare, tightening even further the thin trap of his mouth. But there was in the man some caution which tempered this fury. He scratched a match along the wall and held it up to his mangled smoke but the thing wouldn't draw and he pitched it away.

Someone outside put his horse into a run and quit town, heading east, in the direction of Arnold's. Dust swept into the alley, buffly coating the dust already fogging the window. The mutter of voices came into this quiet and Sam Church growled, "Your time's runnin' out." Then, because he was a man with an unbridled temper, Church permitted himself one additional remark. "You're dead on your feet and ain't got sense enough to know it."

Frank stepped out the door, putting a wall to his back. "Sam, unbuckle that gun belt. Jail's your next stop. For packin' a weapon in a place that sells rotgut. Drop the belt and start hiking."

Old Sam's eyes whipped to Gurden. But the saloonman said:

"Count me out of this, Frank."

Church's face was livid. The upper half of him tipped. The stiffened fingers of his right hand suddenly tensed.

"When you draw that iron you're dead," Frank said.

A trapped desperation brought the bones of Church's face into more vivid prominence. Passion clawed at his guards, the violent urge to defy Frank – but doubt crept in and shame twisted his cheeks and not all his fury could push the hand to his gun.

"Shuck the belt," Frank said, "and let's get started."

Visibly trembling, the old man obeyed. The still-sheathed pistol thumped the floor. Church stared bitterly. Gurden nursed his hate in silence. Church cried in a high half-strangled voice, "When my son learns of this –"

"I'm counting on it." Frank smiled, and scooped up the dropped belt. "Take the side door. I'll be right behind you."

The whole street appeared to be watching as Frank, following Church, stepped out of the alley, got hold of the mare's reins and prodded the second largest owner in the country over to the jail. The stillness was funereal. Out of the corner of an eye Frank saw Krantz's dropped jaw, the sour smile of Wolverton; and was almost across the width of the road before the storekeeper recovered enough to call out. Frank, paying no attention, tossed the mare's reins across the pole of the jail tie-rack, and with gun still in hand followed old Sam into the building.

Kimberland's foreman, Bill Grace, looked up from his perch on Frank's desk, stare inscrutable. Gradually it widened as he took in the meaning of Frank's leveled pistol.

Frank tossed Church's belt into an out-of-reach corner. "Good place for yours, Bill," he said, waggling the six-shooter. "I'm sorry about this, Bill, but right now I can't afford to have you underfoot."

The man got red in the face and began to swell up like a poisoned pup.

"Save it for the Judge," Frank said. "You'll look an awful fool if I have to ventilate both ears."

Bill Grace shut his choppers and uncinched his belt. He slammed it down on the desk and considered the marshal with a look of pure venom. Frank only grinned and tiredly waved him and Church down the corridor.

After fastening them in across the aisle from the others, Frank went back and picked up the two belts, dumping all the cartridges out of their loops and emptying both pistols, same caliber as Will's. He stowed these loads in his pockets and took a look at his watch. Twenty minutes of six. So far he'd been lucky. He didn't look for it to hold.

Will's pistol was a Peacemaker, same as the pair he'd just dropped into the drawer. The model was in much favor. Like the .44/40 Winchester, it shot a .44 caliber bullet weighing 200 grains, propelled by 40 grains of black powder, allowing one belt to carry the loads for both weapons, the only hitch being you had to stick to black powder.

Frank punched the empties out of Will's gun. Someone would sure as hell bring Old Judge into this with a writ to get some of these prisoners sprung. The keys were with Danny Settles and this whole deal might be wound up before anyone happened to think about that. True, the jail might be wrecked. So might South Fork, but it was a heap less likely with these boys in cold storage.

Fed up with their racket Frank got up and slammed the corridor door. This cut it down somewhat and he was pushing fresh loads into Will Church's pistol when Krantz's shape cut off the outside light.

"What you got in your ears? I like to yelled mineself hoarse," he wheezed, mopping his baldness with a limp bandanna. "Vot a blace! Too hot mit der sun und too verdammt cold vit'out it!" He blew irascibly through pursed lips and passed the damp cloth over the rasp of his cheeks. Scowling, he said, "You von't like this."

Frank thrust Will's sixshooter into his pants. "You've come for the badge, I guess."

"Badge! Is about this Kelly. Your friend he vas, hein? Mr. Holliday vants to know vill you stand goot for his burying?"

166

Frank looked at him blankly. "You trying to tell me Kelly's dead?"

"Ass a herringk – Blease! My arm iss not rubber boots." He massaged the limb gingerly. "He vas found on the road to Wega. One off dem trailherders found him. He vas shot in der back."

Kelly dead! It didn't make sense until Frank remembered the message Danny'd given him from Sleight-of-Hand Willie, the Opal's piano man. *Tell him Kelly is into some kind of deal with Gurden.* And Kelly, by that kid, had sent a note asking Frank to meet him – and later had beckoned Frank urgently from the stage barn.

It all added up. Kelly had tried to warn him and, when he couldn't, had got scared and run for it. But what had there been to warn? And then Frank had it. *Tularosa!*

Something came over Frank then and he got up with an oath. Lifting the storekeeper out of his path, he rushed into the street. W. T.'s saddled black was in front of the hotel and Frank cut that way, breaking into a run. He took the steps three at a crack and crossed the porch at one stride. The clerk, frightened and paling, shrank back into his clothes. "What room's she got?" Frank growled, looking wicked.

"T-T-Twelve."

Frank dived for the stairs, making noise enough for a band of wild horses. At the top, breathing hard, he caught hold of the bannister, spotted the number and was lifting his fist to bring it down on the panel when the door was pulled open. Frank, swearing, commenced to back off.

Honey looked at him coldly. "What is it now? I thought another stampede must be loose on the town."

Frank dragged off his hat. "I guess I got the wrong room."

Honey's eyes looked him over like a horse up at auction. "If you came to patch it up you're wasting your time," she said, closing the door.

Frank clapped on his hat and dubiously eyed the line of shut doors. He was thinking of going down for another try at the clerk when a door was pulled open a couple of yards to the left.

"Were you hunting me?" Sandrey asked.

Frank looked powerfully relieved. He hadn't realized what a strain he'd been under until he saw her standing there, unharmed.

He said, "Whew!" and then grinned. But she didn't grin back and Frank, turning sober, decided she hadn't much call to like him and no call at all to let him inside. "If we could talk for a couple of minutes," he said, and she surprised him by moving aside.

He went in and she closed the door, putting the backs of her shoulders against it, gravely regarding him.

Many washings had tightened the thin stuff of her dress. She seemed thinner than he'd remembered, like maybe she hadn't been eating too good. The waning light from the window put hollows in her cheeks. One hand went up to the red mop of her hair and she appeared of a sudden to be breathing more deeply. All he could think about now was her nearness, the feel of her pulled hard against him at Brackley's.

"Wouldn't you like to sit down?" She moved away from the door. "Take that chair. I can perch on the bed."

She didn't seem bothered or much put out by him being here. He remembered Sam Church's words but her eyes watched him straightly; she was more composed than he was. He suddenly reached out, catching hold of her shoulder.

He couldn't make anything out of her look. The warm aliveness of her flesh soaked up into his fingers and he jerked the hand away. A saloon slut, Church had called her. Frank didn't know whether he hated her most or the man who ha 'ned her. She said:

"I thought you said you wanted to talk to me?"

He told her in a stone-cold voice what had been going on, about the railroad and Kimberland, Gurden, all the rest of it.

"And you've got Kimberland's foreman and Sam Church in jail. Of course you know you can't hold them.

"I'll hold them," Frank said, "or long enough anyway to get this deal straightened out."

"What will you do?"

"I jailed Sam Church to put young Will where I can grab him."

"Somebody'll carry him word but he won't come alone."

"That's all right." Frank took a turn. "Having his right bower in clink ought to slow Kimberland down some."

"I can't see Gurden riding tamely out of the picture. Especially if, as you seem to believe, he was hatching some kind of crooked deal with that road scout. And then he's got that forged quitclaim. Or, rather, *if* he's got –"

"He doesn't know about you, does he?" This was what had brought Frank over here, the fear that Gurden knew and might have turned Tularosa loose on her.

"I haven't seen Gurden," she said, "but

if he's the same Chip Gurden who owned the Red Quail over at Brady it's not likely he'll have forgotten me. I used to sing there," she added, returning his stare with a look half defiant.

"Brackley know that?"

There was no humor in Sandrey's smile, but it was Frank who seemed uncomfortable.

"Anyway," he said, too hurriedly and with too much emphasis, "what I meant was does Gurden know about you and Brackley?"

Sandrey, watching him, shrugged. "Does it matter?"

Frank felt the need to square himself but couldn't find the words, tangled up like he was; and the girl presently said, "Gurden's not going to beat me out of that place – or Church, either. I'll find somebody –" She broke off and said, "What makes you think jailing Sam will fetch Will in?"

"He might leave his old man stew for a while, but those three hardcases I've latched onto is something else again. He's got to bust those fellers out or he'll find himself without any hands."

"He must have other –"

"He's got others, all right. It's a matter of salt," Frank said, "of principle. When a man hires out his guns he expects the backing of whoever he's working for. It's part of the code. Will has got to come through for these boys or lose the rest of them."

Frank looked around. He saw the road scout's pistol, at least he imagined it was his, beside the washbowl on the chest of drawers. "Keep that thing handy and stay in this room. Don't open for anyone. Understand?" He waited till she nodded, and then went into the hall, pulling the door shut after him. "Shove that chair under the knob."

"Frank –"

He started down the stairs, glad to be quit of any hold she had on him, relieved to get away from those too-steady eyes. Still scowling at tangled emotions, he found Wolverton and Krantz staring out of the lobby.

Frank said, "Anyone seen Arnold?" and came off the stairs while they were shaking hands. McFell, of the Flag, came in, looking curious, and a jabbering came with him out of the street. Frank said to McFell, "That trail boss around?"

"Can't prove it. Last I heard they'd moved onto Bar 40...." He threw a look over his shoulder and stepped away from the door.

W. T. Kimberland stepped in, saw Frank and strode toward him. "Frank! You've got to do something. This situation's intolerable!"

"You referring to Bill Grace?"

The rancher's mouth shaped the name as though it were some kind of edible; then his eyes began to stretch. He chewed at his lip. Frank watched coldly and Kimberland said, "You might remember how you come to be packing that –" and let it die. A silence enveloped them and grew and reached out to embrace the whole dimensions of the room. Something broke in Kimberland – you could see it run through him like undermined timbers falling after a trembler. The harsh lines of his face were like folds seen through water; and Frank wondered on what sort of facts the cowman's rep had been founded. It was like watching a landmark crack up, he thought bitterly.

W. T. Kimberland's eyes lowered. His clothes seemed too big for him. "I've been framed," he said thickly.

Frank said, "At least you know where I stand."

"You've got to believe me!" Sweat was on Kimberland's face like a dew. "I've done a few things –"

"Like getting rid of Brackley?"

Kimberland hung there. He couldn't get the words out.

There was contempt in Frank's stare. "You put that killer up to it."

"Frank, as God is my witness – I haven't spoken ten words to Tularosa in my life."

"What was Bill Grace supposed to do?"

The rancher's glance squirmed away. "I – he wasn't supposed to do anything."

"I've made sure he won't. If you're in a bind why don't you go to your friends – all those fine ranchers you've led around by the nose?"

The man stared at him numbly.

Frank said at last, "What do you want me to do?"

"Stay out of this. Don't push –"

"First you tell me I've got to do something. Now you want me to stay out of it. Don't you know your own mind?"

The man's look was gray with pleading. "You've let Tularosa go. Can't you do as much for Grace?" He hauled breath into him. "Give me a chance, man! I'll take my losses. I'll stay off the Bench. I'll –"

Frank's grim look stayed the flood of easy assurances. "Will you send your crew to protect those people?"

Kimberland groaned. "Do I have your strict promise –"

"You don't have any kind of promise. You're on probation. What happens to you will depend on the rest of it. On what I think *ought* to happen."

174

Kimberland looked his full age in that moment. "You don't leave me much choice." He scrubbed a hand over his face. "I was a big man this morning; I'll be lucky tomorrow if I've still got a horse. All right." He turned to the door. "I'll do what I can." He went out through dead quiet.

"Py Gott!" Krantz exclaimed, staring unbelievably at Wolverton. Frank quit their company. McFell, staring after him, cleared his throat, shook his head. It was Wolverton who said, "Now we've seen – *everything!*"

There was quite a passel of men on the street, Frank discovered. Quite a bunch right in front of him, motionless, watching him. Kimberland's black was gone from the hitchrail. The sun was gone, too. Down across from the New York Cafe the stage company flunkeys were leading out fresh horses. Frank prowled a glance at the men grouped in front of him. "Any of you care to volunteer for a little duty?"

A couple shuffled their feet. Two or three grinned derisively. But finally one of them, flushing a little, asked to be told what Frank had in mind. "Well," Frank said, "it's like this," and told them what Will Church was up to. "I've got three of his bunch locked up in the pokey – leastways I guess they're a part of his outfit. If they are, it stands to reason

175

he's going to try to bust them out. He may bring some help. I want to lay hold of him on account of that road scout being killed."

Several men exchanged looks. These drew off to one side where they stood muttering a moment. Then one of them asked, "We git paid for this deal?"

"Sure you'll be paid. You'll be full-time deputies for as long as you're needed. How about you?" he said to the blacksmith.

The smith looked around and reluctantly nodded. "Expect I owe you that much, lettin' that feller get away with that wheel." He moved over with the others.

Frank said to a leather-cheeked man, "How about you?"

"Ain't got no rifle."

"Plenty in my office. Plenty of cartridges too."

"I dunno. My ol' woman –"

"Before I swear you in," Frank told the others, "I suppose you should know there's one other thing I may be needing your help with. Tularosa's still loose and –"

"No!" the smith growled, glaring up at him. "I don't want no truck with that damned killer!" He wheeled away, glowering. The other volunteers looked at Frank with stricken faces. "You were hellbent to hang him last night," he reminded them. But

176

last night wasn't now and Tularosa lying unconscious was a totally different story from this killer at bay with guns in his fists. "Not me!" someone gasped, and they melted away.

Frank, squaring his shoulders, headed for Gurden's alone.

CHAPTER FOURTEEN

Chavez, on his horse and still toting his shotgun, angled into the street towing Frank's blue roan mare. Frank shook his head but the Mexican came on, grinding an elbow against his star.

"You stubborn damn peon," Frank growled at him, "stay out of this."

Chavez's teeth made a paler streak against his face. He cupped a hand beside his ear and Frank, glancing back, could see that the stage was about ready to roll. He pulled up to give Gurden a chance to get on it, if he was going to. "I'll keep 'em off your back," Chavez said, and rode off to put the horses behind the wall of the gun shop.

Frank's eyes prowled the face of the Opal. The drawstrings of time were tightening night's shadows, deepening their encroachment. No light showed back of Chip's windows. The Blue Flag was lit up and there were lights in other places, including the stage depot.

He saw Chavez striding toward him and sent him down to check the passengers. Gurden wasn't likely to be making the trip but Frank supposed he'd better wait until the stage had departed. Sending Chavez over there would probably keep the Mexican out of this.

As Frank waited he seemed to catch the mutter of hoofs. Quite a number of notions were keeping him company, few of a nature that would help him relax. The scattered lights of the town intensified the obscurity of blackness untouched by them. The face of Sandrey came into Frank's mind; he heard the driver climbing up to his seat, heard him kick off the brake and yell to his horses. There was the crack of the whip.

Chavez called, "No go," and Frank drew Church's gun. Gurden had had plenty of time to get set for this. There was nothing Frank could do now but walk into it.

Queer how swiftly the street had been deserted. The whole town was watching him now back of windows, in the shelter of doorways. Frank didn't too bitterly blame them. He was paid to take chances.

He stepped out of the shadows. Alertly scanning the Opal's dark front, he saw a shape duck across the boards in front of the Blue Flag and snatch at the reins of a tied pinto horse. The paint sat back, but cursing and hauling finally overcame its stubbornness and its owner pulled it into the safety of the Blue Flag.

The breeze slapped at Frank's coat and was like cold fingers at his forehead and throat. Each step he took required a mental effort. He had always figured walking to be entirely automatic and so was doubly astonished to find each taken stride a victory, each yard of gained progress an unmistakable triumph. The doors of the Opal were just ahead of him now. Another six strides would put him onto the porch.

Arnold, leaving Frank after the lynching of Danny Settles, prowled the town by himself for a while, poking through alleys, peering in through the windows of locked-up buildings, touring Minnie's, the Flag, the stage barn and Fentriss'. He spent a good deal of time before reaching the conclusion which had been forced upon Frank – that in a place like South Fork no man, singlehanded, could hope to run down a free wheeling sidewinder who was making it his business to keep out of the way.

But the rancher had resources not available to Frank and, once he'd been convinced of the fruitlessness of this, he got his horse and left town. It was Arnold's departure the marshal heard when he went into Gurden's office after Sam Church.

Arnold came to the river and rode over the rattling planks of the bridge. Abbie Burks rode with him and he made good time. It was barely six when he swung down at headquarters and set up a yell which brought his crew on the run. Arnold stripped his horse, saddled a fresh one. Inside twenty minutes, armed and mounted, they were riding.

Sandrey, after Frank went down the stairs, stood for some minutes facing the door without seeing it. Not recalling Frank's instructions concerning the chair she went over to the chest and stared into the cracked glass above it. Turning, she moved over to the window, observing how near night had come while she'd been up here. She saw Frank's features against the mauve shadows, the striking force of his stare trying to hide its bleak hunger. While she did not particularly like what she had glimpsed, the fact remained that he'd been concerned enough to come up here in spite of what someone had obviously told him.

She was honest enough to admit the man attracted her, but she'd come to this place on a hunt for security which she'd learned to believe was more important to a woman than any other thing.

She took a turn about the room and tried to see this in a practical manner. She'd come through a hard school and knew how treacherous was emotion. She could have Frank, she was sure of it; but she wouldn't get security. He had no money and poor prospects of ever latching onto any. He had the worst kind of job imaginable, a constant nightmare of suspense which she had no intention of living with. What else did he know? Punching cattle? Thirty dollars a month! Maybe sixty for a man who finally got to be a range boss. It was impossible, she thought, and went and stood again by the window.

The shadows were deeper now. Lamplight gleamed from a dozen scattered openings and the street looked deserted. She heard the stage roll out of town and smelled its dust and saw a man dive out of the Flag and another step out of the gloom near the Opal as somebody cried, "No go."

Unaccountably her eyes stayed with the man approaching Gurden's. It was so dark she couldn't make out the batwings but as he stepped onto the Opal's porch Sandrey suddenly knew that this man was Frank Carrico.

By the chill in the air Frank knew he was sweating. He transferred Church's gun to his left hand and wiped his right against his leg and took the gun back into it again. He was positive Gurden was in there. Chip was not the kind to throw away an advantage.

Frank felt for the walk with the toe of his boot and stepped up and came onto the planks of the porch. The hair began to prickle at the back of his neck. He felt his stomach muscles knotting. Never in his life had he so badly wanted to run. His mouth was dry. He had to stop and consciously moisten it. "Chip –" He put more strength into his voice: "Chip, I'm coming in."

A loose blind flapped off yonder and somewhere a dog howled. Frank could hear the creak of timbers, the tiny groan of the breeze curling round the eaves. This would be a hard winter, it was coming too slow. The crackle of paper whirled away up some alley, every slap of its racket tearing into Frank like splinters.

He struck the doors and went through, crouching low. A gun roared dead ahead, sending up its bright muzzle flash. Frank stepped widely to the right even while it was fading, and again as the gun went still. It was all he could do to keep the squeeze off his trigger.

Quiet regathered its hold and outside there was a restive stamping of horses which bothered Frank vaguely without his quite knowing why. There was a mumble of voice sound too low to untangle. The strike of shod hoofs went away through the dust and the wind came again with a rattle of sashes. The stillness thickened about Frank and the steady working of the clock over the bar beat out the passing time with a measured rhythm which became intolerable. Someone's shout carried over the street but Frank stayed in his tracks and breathed through his mouth. It was inconceivable that Gurden would brace him without another gun hidden someplace. Frank had to know where it was.

Patience paid off. What sounded like a hat struck and fell somewhere to the right of him. Strangely cool now Frank grinned. The failure of the ruse to draw his fire loosened other sounds. The man who had done the shooting let his breath out, moved a little. Frank placed him behind the bar and considered his guess confirmed when a glass shattered back of him. A second glass hit one of the batwings, fell to the floor without breaking and rolled.

"Hell," Mousetrap said, disgusted, "I got him."

The clock ticked on. Mousetrap, moving around behind the bar, began to poke the spent shells from his six-shooter. "Want I should light a lamp?"

Gurden, Frank thought, would have liked nothing better but wasn't about to invite Frank's fire by replying. He was the cagey one; not in the class with Draicup's gunfighter, but even a small rattlesnake can kill. Until Frank could locate Chip Gurden he was stymied. If he fired at the bouncer the saloon boss would get him. It was too sure to doubt. It was the reason why Gurden had fetched Mousetrap into this – a beautiful decoy. Expendable gun bait.

Frank could hear the small sounds of Mousetrap reloading. These quit, and wind scratched across the black paper of the roof. The sound of the clock continued to hammer Frank's skull. Impatience rowelled him. Strain made his eyes burn.

Mousetrap said, "Well – here goes," and

dragged a match across the bar. Before his hand reached the end of its swipe Gurden was driving his lead at Frank, too frantic and too fast, gambling on percentage as he had done all his life.

The first slug cuffed Frank's hat. The next twitched the upturned collar of his jacket, pushing him out of his crouch. He squatted, spotting Gurden behind an overturned table. Frank took his time, caring nothing about Mousetrap, closing his mind to the lead slapping around him. When he finally squeezed trigger Gurden straightened and pitched headlong.

Frank spun then, covering the bar, emptying the gun in a definite pattern, exploding four cartridges before the wild clatter of the bouncer's spooked flight. He felt the air from a door and stood, locked in violence, hearing an outside gun beating into the echoes and a sudden high yell that went cracked in the middle and was drowned in other firing.

Chavez, of course. But Chavez had a sawed-off and this racket came from saddle guns. Frank, remembering the horse sounds, added it up as either Lassiter's trail crew or Will Church and his rustlers. It was like Will, shooting from the dark, not caring who or what he hit. Will, all right – he'd

185

probably taken over the town. But where was Chavez?

More firing broke out, a scattered volley of shots, not as near as those last had been. Surprised yells and cursing. And now, staring out of the Opal's front windows, Frank could see by the flashes that Will Church had his hands full. Will's bunch had lost control of their trap and now they found themselves caught in its jaws. From both sides of the street, from broken windows and door holes and the black slots of alleys, guns were pinning them down in a murderous crossfire.

Frank refilled Church's empty pistol and now remembered the rifle Gurden had left behind the bar, the .44/40 Frank had dropped here last night. He got it and checked it and filled it from his pockets and ran back through the batwings. A dark blob of horses were being hustled from the livery. Levering a shell into position Frank dropped the man who had hold of them. From a squealing pitching tangle the horses broke in every direction. Will's men, running to mount them, were caught flat-footed in the street without cover.

"Throw down your guns!" Chavez, that was.

Frank couldn't see him but caught the

lifting glint of a gun barrel of a Church man, and fired just above it and saw a bent shadow reel away from its surroundings. A shotgun went off *prr-u-mph!* with both barrels. Three shapes lurched out of that howling commotion, and the rest yelled for quarter.

Frank ran into the street and the wind whirling down out of the north tore his hat away. Chavez came out of the gloom with his Greener, limping a little, paying no attention to Frank's allusions to his ancestry. "It's a wonder," Frank said, "they didn't cut you into gun patches!"

The Mexican grinned. "Nobody uses gun patches any more." He laughed, full-throated, pounding a fist at Frank's kidney. "We got 'em, boy – we done it!"

Frank followed him, tagging after the rest, fastening his jacket against the bite of the wind. Like Chavez he was excited, but sober too, his mind filled darkly with the remembrance of falling men; moreover, by a disquieting hunch the kingpin hand of this deal had not been played.

Krantz came up, catching and wringing Frank's hand, short of breath but vastly beaming in the satisfaction of achievement. "Ach," he wheezed, "vot a pizness! Who sayss shopkeepers von't fight!"

Frank nodded. "You done a bangup job."

187

He disengaged his fist. His glance, still uneasy, kept a roving watch.

He was prowling the edge of things seen but not definable. He even had the weird notion someone was following him although nothing he tried disclosed any sign of this.

He pushed into the crowd surrounding Church's crew. "Chavez," he called, "where've you put Tularosa?"

The deputy frowned. "Didn't bag him." Worried stares replaced some of the grins in Frank's vicinity and the crowd's enthusiasm took a noticeable slump. "What's more," Chavez said, "we didn't lay hold of Will, either. All we got was the scrapin's."

Frank grabbed the first dozen men he could lay hands on and sent them off to round up the loose horses. "Get 'em all," he said grimly, "including those at the tie-racks. We don't stop this here we never will without more killing."

He was afraid in his own mind the time was already past when shutting the stable was going to do much good. He detailed other men to close-herd the prisoners and sent Chavez over to keep an eye on the jail. Bernie, Krantz and Wolverton he put to gathering weapons. "Go through the Opal, too, while you're at it. Take everything over to your place, Krantz, and –"

"Say, Frank," one of the unconscripted townsmen called, "this bunch of sidewinders Church fetched down on us looks just about ready for a jig on a rope."

Frank turned on him, furious. "Next feller mentions rope is going to jail!"

The man slunk away. Frank got some hard looks. He considered the prisoners but turned away without speaking. They probably had no more idea where their boss was than Frank had. If Will had got a horse he might be halfway to Dallas.

Frank looked for the pair Chavez had left by Bernie's but the passage was empty. The blacksmith, coming up, tapped Frank on the shoulder. "If you're lookin' fer them broncs, I seen Ben leadin' them off with some others. Boys're holdin' 'em all in one of them pens back of the livery."

Frank eyed the Sharps the smith was toting and told him to go over and see that they stayed there. He looked around him, still worried, and was about to head for the hotel to check on Sandrey when he thought he saw movement in the slot separating Ben's place from the barber shop. When he looked more carefully he guessed he had been mistaken. No reason for Will to be back there – nor anyone else, he told himself sourly. Keyed up like he was a man could see just

189

about anything. He went on a few steps then swung around and cut over.

He stopped a moment in the deeper gloom of Ben's overhang, thinking the rifle might be more of a nuisance than help in close quarters. While he was debating abandoning it he got the feeling again of eyes boring into him and looked edgily around, discovering nothing.

Keeping hold of the Winchester, Frank stepped into the alley. In the murk he paused, listening, testing the place for whatever it might tell him. But with all that wind he finally gave up.

Lifting Will's pistol from his holster he again stepped ahead. Midway through it occurred to him young Church might have arranged to play decoy on the chance of pulling Frank into a bind. This didn't seem too likely. He would have had to got hold of Tularosa; seeking and finding that fellow weren't the same. The man was like a damn wolf!

Frank stopped in his tracks. He'd heard nothing ahead of him or anything behind but the safety mechanism of primitive instincts was sounding an alarm.

He gripped the pistol with tightening fingers, taking comfort in the feel of it. Bending, he put the rifle down, trying from this angle to catch a larger view. He didn't discover anything and, straightening, went on, doubly conscious of the risk of sending a stray tin clattering. He couldn't be sure he had reloaded. Ten steps from the end of the passage he decided it was better to be certain than sorry.

He crouched again, forced to bring both hands to the task. The gun had five rounds in it. He glanced once more front and back and had just flicked open the loading gate to put one under the hammer when sudden awareness of danger brought his eyes up, rounding, frantic.

All his reflexes locked, seeing that shape so startlingly in front of him. He presently realized the fellow had his back to him, had ducked into the slot to conceal himself from something else. Even as this came to Frank the man in front of him wheeled and froze, stiff with shock.

Now that Frank could see in this gloom, enough reflected light reached the man from the street to reveal Will Church in the startled blob of those gone-awry features.

Church, recovering, stumbled backward, striving to reach shelter even as he brought up his hand. With Frank desperately scrabbling to get his gun into action, Church backed out of the alley, the walls briefly lighting to the flash of his fire.

The double concussion hammered Frank to the ground. It was like a white-hot iron had touched him. After that he lost track. He knew a gun was still pounding but he didn't feel the bullets. Too numbed, he supposed; and got his hands on the pistol.

He pushed his chest off the ground and there was nothing to shoot at. Will was down, writhing, groaning. Frank thought the fool had shot himself – until his widening stare found the girl.

He licked cracked lips. He had to shape them twice before her name got past the dryness of his throat. Then he thought she didn't hear it.

But this was shock, delayed reaction. Her head came around as he was getting to his feet. She dropped Fles' gun and rushed into Frank's arms.

He had told her to stay in the hotel, to keep her door shut, but "Sandrey – Sandrey!" was all he could say. She seemed content; and it came over Frank that achieving social acceptance in the eyes of Kimberland and people like the Churches lacked a long way of being as important to a man as hooking up with a competent woman.

Now the crowd drawn by the shots was

all around them, shoving and jostling for a look at Will Church. Sandrey said, hanging onto Frank, "When I couldn't stand worrying about this fellow any longer I left the hotel. I saw Will Church slip into this alley. Then I saw Frank starting over here. I knew he was after Church. I had that road scout's gun; I went round the other side." She paused to say thoughtfully, "Church didn't know about Frank, I guess. Time Church got to the back I wasn't far off, heading toward him. I expect he heard me, got rattled, ducked back and saw Frank."

"I was loadin' his pistol," Frank said disgustedly.

Sandrey squeezed his arm. "I didn't know what to do. I was practically on top of him when Church brought his gun up. I guess I kind of went out of my head. Next I knew, Church was down and –"

"Yah," said Councilman Krantz. "Frank couldn't done no different. Justifiable homicide. Ve got a goot marshal. Ve goin' to raise his pay –"

"Give the star to Chavez," Frank said. "I'm getting hitched."

The storekeeper's shrewd eyes jumped to Sandrey and back again. "Veddingk bells, iss it? Ve vill gif you a bonus!"

Frank went over and bent down beside

Will, others crowding around. Will Church wasn't going to make it. Frank got up. "Expect we could use that bonus, me and Sandrey, but –" Frank broke off. "Where is she?"

The whole crowd looked around, everyone staring toward the mouth of the passage. The pit of Frank's belly knotted and the cold got into the marrow of his bones. Backing into the comparative brightness of the street were two locked shapes.

Tularosa!

"Keep back if you want this frail to stay healthy!"

The man's left arm was wrapped around Sandrey's waist, making a shield of her. Frank was still holding the loaded pistol but might just as well have tried to attack with his teeth. As the outlaw backed into the shadows, Frank, unable longer to contain himself, started after them. The girl redoubled her struggles, making the gunfighter lurch with her efforts. Flame, like a snake, darted out of his hand. Frank, flung half around, crashed into the wall. When he got himself off it his left arm hung useless. He was barely in time to see Tularosa disappear with the girl in the direction of the river.

Frank stumbled into the street. Someone yelled from the darkness: "Arnold –

Arnold!" and a thunder of hoofs swept over the bridge. Cut off, Tularosa came dragging the girl back, trying to make it to the livery. Frank saw Arnold's crew riding hellity-larrup but it was plain Tularosa would get under cover before they'd be able to come into range. The blacksmith with his Sharps was somewhere back of the stable but this was Frank's job and that girl out there was Sandrey.

"Now, Frank – now!" she cried, and hauled her feet up, folding. The full weight of her, hanging from the killer's arm, pulled him off balance and he had to let go of her.

Frank fired two shots and saw Tularosa stagger. He fell onto a knee and Frank emptied his gun.

Krantz came up, fairly bursting with excitement. "A goot marshal! Py Gott! Ve gif you two bonus!"